MAID
FOR IT

JAMIE SUMNER

ATHENEUM BOOKS FOR YOUNG READERS
New York   London   Toronto   Sydney   New Delhi

ATHENEUM BOOKS FOR YOUNG READERS

An imprint of Simon & Schuster Children's Publishing Division

1230 Avenue of the Americas, New York, New York 10020

This book is a work of fiction. Any references to historical events, real people, or real places are used fictitiously. Other names, characters, places, and events are products of the author's imagination, and any resemblance to actual events or places or persons, living or dead, is entirely coincidental.

Text © 2023 by Jamie Sumner

Jacket illustration © 2023 by Jacqueline Li

Jacket design by Karyn Lee © 2023 by Simon & Schuster, Inc.

All rights reserved, including the right of reproduction in whole or in part in any form.

ATHENEUM BOOKS FOR YOUNG READERS is a registered trademark of Simon & Schuster, Inc. Atheneum logo is a trademark of Simon & Schuster, Inc.

For information about special discounts for bulk purchases, please contact Simon & Schuster Special Sales at 1-866-506-1949 or business@simonandschuster.com.

The Simon & Schuster Speakers Bureau can bring authors to your live event. For more information or to book an event, contact the Simon & Schuster Speakers Bureau at 1-866-248-3049 or visit our website at www.simonspeakers.com.

Interior design by Jacquelynne Hudson-Underwood

The text for this book was set in Adobe Caslon Pro.

Manufactured in the United States of America

0723 FFG

First Edition

10 9 8 7 6 5 4 3 2 1

Library of Congress Cataloging-in-Publication Data

Names: Sumner, Jamie, author.

Title: Maid for it / Jamie Sumner.

Description: First edition. | New York : Atheneum Books for Young Readers, [2023] | Audience: Ages 10 and Up. | Summary: When her mother is injured in a car accident, twelve-year-old Franny tries to keep their fragile world intact by taking over her mom's cleaning jobs.

Identifiers: LCCN 2022053314 | ISBN 9781665905770 (hardcover) | ISBN 9781665905794 (ebook)

Subjects: CYAC: Mothers and daughters—Fiction. | Family problems—Fiction. | Drug addiction—Fiction. | House cleaning—Fiction.

Classification: LCC PZ7.1.S8545 Mai 2023 | DDC [Fic]—dc23

LC record available at https://lccn.loc.gov/2022053314

FOR K. S.
YOU ARE MISSED

1
EVERYTHING'S FINE

THE CALL COMES OVER the loudspeaker twenty-three minutes into math class. Not at the end. That's how I know it's bad. Teachers protect class time like it's an endangered species. So when Mrs. Pack squawks over the intercom, "Franny Bishop to the principal's office. *Immediately*," I know it's emergency-level terrible. I know because I've been here before.

Bending under the table to grab my bag is my first mistake. My defenses are down, or more like they're pointed somewhere else, and Sloan senses it, like any predator in the wilds of middle school. She kicks my old JanSport all the way to the other side of the table, out of reach. I scoot like a crab and grab it. She laughs, but I shake it off. Because I have to. Because whatever's waiting for me in the office has to be way worse than Sloan. Mistake number two would be letting her get to me when there is so much more badness ahead.

Mr. Jamison, my math teacher, gives me a little salute

on the way out. With my table down from three to two, his probability activity isn't going to work. I realize it before he does, which is a gold star no one but me will ever see. I get an itch of guilt because I've ruined the next twenty-two minutes of class for him by leaving, but I keep my feet shuffling forward and out the door because that's all I can do. Sloan shoots me a mock salute behind Mr. Jamison's back and a cheery fake smile just before the door shuts.

My shoes squeak too loud on the tile floor. I freeze in the middle of the hallway.

It's been three years, our longest stretch yet. I thought we were really in the clear, in the clean camp for good. No more pills. We were supposed to be done. She promised.

I had my first walk like this in kindergarten in a different school in a different state. The secretary called me halfway through circle time. I skipped down the yellow halls like I was on my way to recess. I didn't know to expect anything bad. I should have. Things had been off for a while, but when you're five, there is no normal other than the one you've always known. How was I supposed to know most moms don't fall asleep in their car in the driveway or space out midsentence over dinner? "Hitting rock bottom" is a stupid saying. There's always farther to fall.

My stomach pinches, so I crouch down next to the water fountain and dig my planner out of my bag. I flip to today to trace the agenda with my fingertip. The list calms me.

TUESDAY, MARCH 4

Leave bologna sandwich in fridge for Mom w/
apple

Lunch—Return *Meet Me at Harry's* to library and
print English paper

1:45 p.m.—English paper due

4:00 p.m.—Help Mimi sort change

4:30 p.m.–6:00 p.m.—homework until Mom gets
home

Dinner—Leftovers?

I cross out *bologna sandwich* with my teal-ink pen. Mom tasks always get teal. I look over the rest and gulp some air until it doesn't hurt in my chest. Maybe this call to the office isn't a big deal. Maybe it's just Mom telling me she picked up another house to clean or another Uber shift and won't be home until late. Except she usually just tells Mimi or leaves a Post-it on our door with a smiley face and a coupon for pizza. I zip the planner back into my bag and tuck my hair behind my ears—it's too long. I make a mental note to write a *real* note to remind Mom to cut it later. Then I stand and order my heart to slow down. It'll be fine. I'm fine. We're fine.

But in the office, Mrs. Pack's face has the crumbly look of wet sand. "Oh, honey," she says, and something inside me collapses.

• • • •

I sit by the baseball field as far away from the school and as close to the main road as I can get so Mimi doesn't have to waste time pulling all the way up to the entrance. It's almost spring, but the wind doesn't care. I shiver in my purple coat.

Mimi drives up to the curb in her old blue pickup truck fifteen minutes later. Fourteen minutes and fifty-five seconds of that I filled with a mental slideshow of worst-case scenarios. Mrs. Pack didn't have much information for me. Only that Mom was in the hospital and Mimi was on her way. Mrs. Pack tucked a Werther's caramel into my pocket and waved like she'd never see me again. For all I know, she won't.

Before Mimi can come to a full stop, I swing open the door. She says "Heyya, girlie" as I jump in and we roll onward. Her face is grim, but her hands aren't shaking on the wheel. I focus on that. Her knuckles are knobby with arthritis, but the big bony hills of them look steady.

We make a left, away from the school and toward the small center of downtown Cedarville. I've been here for a while now, and it's still strange to see the dark windows of the antiques store and the old hardware store butting up against Starbucks and Whole Foods. Mimi hates it. She never comes this way if she can help it. Whenever I ride with her to the bank, she'll point out a new chain store and mutter "gentrification" like it's a dirty word. I thought gentrifying meant making something old better again, but Mimi sees it as an invasion of her territory. I don't know what she expects. Cedarville might be small, but it's one exit from a truck stop and two from the airport. The world was going to find it eventually.

"What'd that Pack lady tell you?" Mimi asks without taking her eyes off the road.

"Not enough. Car accident. Mom's in the hospital." I shove my hands in my pockets. It's not like I needed all the details, but she didn't even say the most important thing: Mom's going to be okay.

Mimi nods. Her short hair, more salt than pepper now, is standing up all over her head. She seems calm, but her hair tells a different story.

"Some idiot turned left on a red. Your mama was on her way to the Ellsworth house for an early start."

"It wasn't her fault?" I ask.

Mimi shoots me a sideways look. "No, love. And the doc said she was wearing her seat belt. Good thing."

Shame smacks me right in the face. I assumed it was Mom's fault. She's always asking me to have a little faith in her. I twist the Werther's candy in my pocket like a worry stone until the wrapper comes off and it sticks to my fingers.

As we pull into visitor parking, I get a good look at the hospital and my heart sinks. It's red brick and only four or five stories. Anything less than ten floors and you lose all credibility. They might as well have taken her to the vet.

Right before we walk out from under the big gray sky and into the lobby, I shoot a prayer like an arrow. *If she's all right,* I say to the higher power Mom is always talking about, *I'll never assume anything's her fault ever again.*

2

ROOMS FOR WAITING

THE EMERGENCY WAITING ROOM SMELLS like disinfectant and vomit and french fries. A handful of people are sprinkled across the rows of nailed-down seats. They keep their distance from one another. In the far corner, a lady holds a trash bag full of ice to her head. Near the front desk, a guy with tissues shoved up his nose leans his head against a woman's shoulder. Before I can look away, he gags and spits into a small paper cup. To my left, someone groans so loud, it has to be fake. We hurry past them all to the check-in desk, where a nurse sits, looking too tired for eleven a.m. on a Tuesday.

"Julia Bishop," Mimi says without any small talk.

The nurse taps on her computer. *Tap-ta-tap-tap.* Little keystrokes that are a map to my mother. I try to breathe deep, but the vomity smell sneaks in and clings to me. Behind us, the faker ends his groan and starts another one.

"She's in surgery," the nurse says after a few more taps. "Second floor. You'll have to go back out these doors and in through the regular entrance. Take the first set of elevators." She points to the exit and we walk back out. I gulp cold air like I'm coming up after a long dive.

This part of the hospital smells like floor cleaner and stale air. Mimi pauses in the lobby and turns in a circle, her beat-up blue suede purse dangling from her fingers. I step in front and lead us to the first set of elevators. When they open, I push the button for the second floor. For better or worse, I can follow directions.

The waiting area for surgery is practically empty, which doesn't seem fair. While other people coast through their regularly planned days, we've been spit out into this room with copies of *People* and *Southern Living* on the tables, and with windows that overlook Walgreens and Sonny's Diner. We take a seat by the wall of windows. Mimi taps her finger on the glass.

"Best milkshakes in town," she says, pointing at Sonny's.

I nod without looking. Mom and I don't go out to eat much. It's too expensive. Usually I cook something from a box or we splurge and order whatever we have a coupon for. An image of Mom's bologna sandwich flopped open in the middle of the road skitters across my brain before I can unthink it. I shudder and curl into myself.

Mimi puts a hand on my back, but neither of us is touchy-feely, so after a second, she removes it and unzips her windbreaker. Underneath, she wears what she calls her uniform—overalls and a sweater. She says no one cares what the old lady at the laundromat wears.

The nurse up here said it would be at least a couple of hours before Mom is out of surgery. High up in one corner of the room a TV mounted on the wall plays some *Law & Order* show on low volume. I tuck my knees under my chin and stare at the splotchy pattern on the carpet—mauve and tan.

"She's stable, Franny," Mimi says after a while. "That's what we're going to hang on to. This wait is both the hardest and easiest part. So you've got to rest your mind and body as best you can before the next bit."

Well, that's as clear as mud. I don't lift my head. I'm used to this kind of stuff from Mimi. As a long-standing member of Alcoholics and Narcotics Anonymous, she's got a whole pile of sayings that could mean everything or nothing, depending on your mood. She pulls a crossword from her purse.

"Want to work a puzzle with me?"

I shake my head. I'm remembering the last hospital stay, three years ago in Memphis. Mimi wasn't there for that one. It wasn't a car accident. It wasn't someone else's fault. And Mom *wasn't* stable. They didn't let me visit her there. I didn't see her again until the rehab center.

I fish my planner out of my bag. It's lunchtime at school. I planned to spend it in the library so I wouldn't have to sit in the cafeteria alone. I don't mind sitting alone, but nobody ever believes that. When the school counselor, Ms. Taylor, spotted me at lunch a few months back, she called me into her office. I didn't even get to finish my peanut butter and banana sandwich.

"Are you lonely, Franny?" she said, steepling her fingers and resting them on her chin like she'd watched too many of those crime dramas.

"No, ma'am."

She tilted her head at me in that way adults do when they think you're lying. "Then why do you sit by yourself in the cafeteria?"

I looked at her for a beat.

"Why do you eat lunch in your office by yourself?" I'd seen her in here with her pasta salad, scrolling on her phone and looking much happier than she did when she had a student across from her.

She blinked but didn't answer, so I picked up my backpack and stood. "Sometimes it's just nice to have a little space."

She hasn't called me back in since.

Four *Law & Order*s later, I remember that waiting room time isn't like regular time. It passes slow and gloopy, like cheap pancake syrup. By now I have missed science and English. This day is beyond saving. I tear the page out of my planner, shred it, and then roll the pieces into little balls and line them up on the windowsill. Organized chaos. It helps pass the time, but it doesn't ease the tightness in my chest. *Is Mom breathing on her own?* The thought makes my throat close up.

I'm reaching for my bottle of water when the doors that lead to the operating rooms swing open and a woman in bright blue scrubs walks toward us. Mimi puts her hand on my back and leaves it there. I get that sensation of falling, like if I look down I'll topple over.

"Naomi Rutherford?"

I look around for someone else.

"That's me," Mimi says. For a second I forgot her real name is Naomi.

The doctor looks at Mom's chart. "You're the emergency contact, but you're not family, is that correct?"

Mimi nods. I also forgot she's not family. Our "family" is back in Memphis, but we don't count them anymore.

"And you're Frances, Julia's daughter?" the doctor asks. When she smiles at me, I see laugh lines.

"It's Franny," I whisper, and my heart stops. Here's the moment I find out if this is the same world I woke up in or not.

"Franny," she says, "I'm Dr. Lipman. Your mom did great. We repaired her femoral shaft fracture"—she taps above her knee—"her thigh bone, using a technique called intramedullary nailing."

I wince at the word "nailing."

"It's not as bad as it sounds. We inserted a metal rod into the canal of the femur. It will keep the bone stable so it can heal. She's lucky it was a clean break. We expect a full recovery in three to four months' time if she follows the prescribed physical therapy." She smiles again, and the laugh lines deepen. "But for tonight, she needs rest. We're keeping her sedated, but you can come see her during visiting hours tomorrow, okay?"

I nod, and all the breaths I'd been holding whoosh out of me. Mimi stands. "Thank you," she says, and her voice cracks. I thought Mimi was uncrackable. I watch her bony hand grip the doctor's, and send an arrow of thanks into the sky. Mom's going to be all right.

3

CLOSED FOR BUSINESS

"THAT'S MORE MILK THAN SHAKE." Mimi points to the puddle in my cup that I'm stirring with a straw.

We picked up Sonny's milkshakes and burgers on the way home. This might be the best strawberry milkshake I've ever had, but I can't taste it. All the relief from finding out Mom's okay evaporated on the ride home. In its place is a boatload of new questions. Tomorrow, I will see Mom. Tomorrow, we will make a plan and get back on track. But which track is it? The one where I make both our lunches and go to school while she cleans houses and drives people around until dinnertime in our little apartment over Mimi's laundromat? How's she going to clean when she can't walk? How's she going to Uber without something to drive?

Mimi scoots back from the green card table that serves as her kitchen/dining/living room table. Her space is no bigger than one of the classrooms at school—it's one room with a kitchenette, a couch, and a twin bed, plus a closet-sized bathroom. That's it. The rest of the first floor is the laundromat.

She says she prefers "monklike living," but I bet she misses the space she lost when we showed up on her doorstep a few years back with a bag of dirty laundry and not much else. I fold a pickle into my burger wrapper and scoot away from the table.

"Honey, I know you're fine on your own, but do you want to stay down here tonight?" she asks, gathering our trash and dumping it in the garbage under the sink. She's going to be smelling pickles all night.

Most adults ask questions that aren't really questions. They are declarative sentences in disguise. But not Mimi. When she asks, she really wants to hear your answer. I know she'd let me go up and sleep in my own space if I wanted to.

I wipe crumbs off the table and nod. I don't want to be alone.

We venture out into the laundromat to see if anyone's midcycle. This late it's usually truckers in the middle of a long haul or third-shift workers from the dog food plant down the road. But tonight the place is empty, so she flips the OPEN sign to CLOSED, double-locks the door, and switches off the fluorescent lights. We are blanketed in darkness, and I feel it heavy on me. She never closes early except on Wednesdays, and that was going on long before we moved here. Tonight, though, is another debt we can't pay.

Back in her apartment I help her make up the couch with yellow-flowered sheets that are thin and soft from years of washing.

"Good night, Franny, love," Mimi says when she comes out of the bathroom in an old T-shirt and men's pajama pants. She stops to smooth a corner of the sheet that has come loose by my foot. It's not quite tucking me in, but it's enough to make my throat close up. I turn my head toward the back of the couch.

"Night, Mimi."

I hear her bed creak as she gets comfortable. The blue light from the neon sign for MIMI'S LAUNDROMAT sneaks in from the window and stretches across the floor.

When Mimi's breathing evens out in sleep, I let the tears come. It feels good and bad at the same time—like ripping the day in my planner to shreds.

After one minute or a million, Mimi whispers, "I'll tell you what I tell your mother: with the new day comes new strength and new thoughts."

So, not asleep, then.

I sniff. "Is that from AA?"

"No, honey, that's Eleanor Roosevelt," Mimi says, and rolls over. "Now get some rest."

I dream of candy—piles of green and yellow SweeTARTS and blue M&M'S and orange Skittles and the long bright pink Good & Plentys that look like they'd be full of goodness but actually taste like licorice-flavored dirt. I'm four, and I've made neat piles of it all on my bedroom floor back in

Memphis—tiny hills of treats, like a mini Willy Wonka village. I tuck my feet underneath my Moana nightgown so I don't accidentally knock into them.

One by one I begin to transfer the candies into one of Mom's thread boxes. It's a big plastic rectangle divided into thirty-two smaller squares—perfect for storing tiny treasures. Each candy gets its own square. I smile to myself. Mom's going to be so excited. It won't all be a big jumble in the Ziploc bag under the sink anymore. Now when she gets up in the middle of the night, it will be easier for her to find what she wants.

Someone reaches over my shoulder and smacks my hand.

"Franny, no!"

My knee knocks into the box. It tips over, and everything goes rolling under the bed and across the floor. A few SweeTARTS land in the yellow glow of my night-light.

Mom grabs me by the shoulders too hard. It hurts. Her nails dig into my skin. My hand is blotchy and stings where she hit it.

"These are not toys!" she cries, her face stretched like when you pull your ponytail too tight. "Never, ever touch these!"

I burst into tears.

I jerk awake and curl into myself. Dumb, dumb, dumb. How dumb was I to ever think pills were candy? What candy ever made you act like that?

4

VISITING HOURS

WEDNESDAY, MARCH 5

Leftover Hamburger Helper in fridge for Mom

Math—ask Mr. Jamison for extra-credit work

Lunch—ask Mr. Jamison if I can do extra-credit
   work in his room instead of cafeteria

After school—help Mom clean @ Mrs. Ivey's

Dinner—tomato soup

"WHAT'S ON THE AGENDA?"

I am awake before the sun, but not before Mimi. She catches me hunched over my planner on the couch. I've already folded the sheets and straightened the cushions. It's like I was never here.

"Nothing," I say, and it's true. Everything I wrote for today was before the accident, back when life *had* a plan. Now math extra credit doesn't matter. The Hamburger Helper can turn to fuzzy mush and it doesn't matter. Mrs. Ivey's house is not getting cleaned today, and it doesn't matter one bit. None of it matters. Because instead of all of that, I am going to the hospital to see Mom.

Mimi eyes me over a cup of coffee so strong, it clears my sinuses from across the room. Her hair is sticking up in all directions, like she's a friendly troll. She checks the clock on the wall, and my insides flip like a pancake. It's 5:50 a.m. Visiting hours don't start until eight. There is so much time to fill and nothing to fill it with.

"How about I get cleaned up and you can help me open the laundromat since school's off the table today?"

I nod. When she disappears into the bathroom, I look down at my planner again. It is purple and sparkly and came with an attached clicky pen you can switch from pink to blue to teal to black ink. Mom and I found it at Dollar General this summer when we were buying a kiddy pool to put on the roof. With a sigh, I draw a big X over the entire day and underneath write *HOSPITAL*.

Opening the laundromat is easy. I've done it so many times, the routine is automatic, like blinking.

Step 1: Check all washers and dryers for leftover clothes and add to the lost and found basket by the front door.

Step 2: Clean all the lint traps in the dryers, twice. Lint is a huge fire hazard. Whenever Mimi pulls a big, matted gray wad from one of the mesh trays, she mutters "kindling" and shakes it at me.

Step 3: Check the change machine to make sure it's full of quarters.

Step 4: Check the detergent and fabric softener in the vending machines to make sure they are full of travel-sized Tide.

Step 5: Sweep under the orange plastic chairs that line the wall to catch all the lint dust bunnies.

Step 6: Flip the sign to OPEN and unlock the door.

When we're done, it's still only 7:05 a.m. We both study the clock for thirteen seconds before Mimi says, "Right," grabs her coat and her keys, and opens the front door. The bell above it jingles. "Come on, honey. Let's go. We'll see if we can't break some rules this morning and sneak in early."

I'm so glad to cheat time that the world goes blurry. I blink back the tears and follow Mimi into the frosty morning.

• • • •

Turns out you *can't* cheat time. And you definitely can't break the visiting-hour rules, according to the coldhearted nurse at the fourth-floor reception desk.

"You'd think they were written in stone and carried down a mountain," Mimi gripes as we retreat to the waiting room, where a few other visitors are reading newspapers or sleeping in chairs.

She sits, but I don't. My body won't let me. I follow the edge of the beige carpet around and around the small room. I have never been good at waiting. I like to be master of my own time, thank you very much. This is unnecessary torture.

At 7:56 a.m., I present myself before the nurse and stare. She is typing on a computer and does not look at me. But I know she sees me. I watch her mistype. Delete. Type again. Delete. When she clears her throat, I think she's going to order me back to my seat like a teacher, but she doesn't. She sighs.

"What was the name, again?"

"Julia Bishop," I whisper. I'm struck shy by her attention.

She taps on her computer.

"Room four-oh-oh-five," she says, then leans over and presses a button. The automatic doors to my right click open. "Go on back."

I check the small digital clock on her desk. It is 7:58 a.m. Victory.

The hospital floor is a maze of hallways that all look the same. Little windows look into each room. Some have their curtains drawn and are as dark as night. At first we turn the wrong way and find ourselves at another nurses' station and have to ask directions. After a few more minutes of confused roaming, we make our way past a coffee and water station with impossibly small foam cups and I spot room 4005. Light streams out the open door.

Half of me wants to run toward it so I can see for myself how Mom really is. But the other half, the half that remembers her last hospital stay, wins. I freeze. Mimi bumps into me with an "oof."

"Honey," she says, after thirty seconds or so of us just standing there while nurses and patients and visitors weave around us, "there is a finite number of steps a person takes in their lifetime. I reckon you ought to use up some more." She tugs my coat. "Come on, now."

"I don't like surprises."

"I know."

"What if the doctor was wrong?" I ask. "What if it's worse than a broken leg?" I don't say, *What if she was high and it really* was *her fault?* I learned a long time ago, you don't ask a question you don't want the answer to.

Mimi looks me straight in the eye, because she's only as tall as me. "Then we'll find out and we'll deal with it, because *that's what we do.*" I don't know if she's answering my question about the leg or the unspoken one. Mimi is spooky like that. It's enough to unlock my knees. I let her lead me down the hall all the way to the open door. And I swallow my panic, because that's what *I* do.

5

THE PAIN SCALE

I GASP. MOM LOOKS LIKE an extra in *Coraline*. Deep-purple bruises make her face blotchy and puffy, and some kind of rash runs across it like terrible confetti. Her blond hair falls in a tangle around her shoulders. *That'll need three shampoos and the Pantene conditioner to sort out,* I think, because my thoughts are all over the place today. Something else is off too. Her head seems naked, and I can't figure out why. . . . Oh, right, she's not wearing a bandana. She *always* wears a bandana. She is my mother and a stranger all at once.

She turns her head slowly, but her voice is a loud exclamation point.

"My baby!"

I shuffle forward. "Hi, Mom."

"Can you believe this?" She gestures at her leg, which I haven't been brave enough to look at yet. I do now. It juts out from under the thin blanket, but it's wrapped in bandages from hip to ankle, so I can't tell much. Compared to the lump that is her other leg, though, it's twice the size.

She laughs when she sees me staring. Her voice sounds . . . wrong, too strong and sweet, like the syrup at the bottom of a snow cone.

Mimi goes around to her far side and places a firm hand on her arm. I'm still afraid to touch her.

"How are you, Jules?" she asks, studying her like the human lie detector she is.

"Oh, I'm good," Mom says, waving her other hand. Her IV swings back and forth. I flinch. It seems like it should hurt, but she doesn't react. I follow the tube up to a bag hanging from a metal pole. It's full of a clear liquid. There's a label, but I wouldn't know what it is, even if I could read it from here. Somewhere inside me, a warning light starts flashing.

Mimi and Mom are still in their staring contest. Eventually Mom's smile slips, and Mimi pulls up a chair.

"'Good' may be an exaggeration," Mom admits.

Mimi nods and leans back.

"Come here, baby," Mom says, and pats the seat on her other side. I move next to her, but I don't sit. Me and the IV bag are having our own staring contest. I point to it.

"What's in here?" I ask.

Before Mom can answer, the doctor from yesterday, Dr. Lipman, walks into the room. Without her blue surgical cap, I can see that her hair is gray. She's older than I thought, close to Mimi's age. But where Mimi is all hard lines and sunspots, this woman is smoothed out—like she's traveled through life on the gentle cycle.

"Hello, Ms. Bishop. How are you doing this morning?"

"I'm good!" Mom says, perky again. Mimi nudges her and Mom rolls her eyes, the first true thing I've seen her do since we got here.

Dr. Lipman says nothing. She sets down her chart at the end of the bed and begins to slowly remove the tape from the bandages on Mom's leg. I look away. The sharp scent of blood and disinfectant finds me anyway.

A few minutes pass as Dr. Lipman gives reassuring murmurs and asks questions like "Can you feel this? What about this? Can you wiggle your toes?"

I turn around again when I hear the rush of water from the sink by the bathroom. Mom's face is gray. She looks wrung out.

Dr. Lipman turns back to us from washing her hands. "Everything looks good. Swelling and drainage from the incision sites are normal. However"—she pauses—"I want to keep you here for another few nights."

I look from Mom to the doctor. Why keep her here longer if everything looks good? Something isn't right.

Dr. Lipman is still talking. "We didn't see any rib fractures on the chest X-ray, but I'd like to order another one for tomorrow, given the force of that airbag and the bruising."

Mom lifts a hand and touches her cheek. The purple

blotches and red rash go all the way down her face and disappear below the neckline of her hospital gown. The airbag—the thing designed to protect her—did *that*? What would she look like if it *hadn't* gone off? My stomach twists and the room spins. I think I'm going to be sick. I grip the bedrail.

"I really think I'm fine," Mom says, aiming her words at me. "I'd like to go home."

Dr. Lipman glances up from her chart. "We need to make sure you are healthy enough to care for yourself safely at home first," she says. "How's your pain? On a scale from zero, no pain at all, to ten, worst possible pain?"

Mom's color has not returned to normal. She looks up at the ceiling like she's thinking, but I know she's pretending. You don't live with a person for twelve years and not learn their tells.

"Oh, four to five, I'd say."

No one speaks, except Mimi, who clicks her tongue so forcefully I'm surprised she doesn't crack a tooth.

"Ms. Bishop," Dr. Lipman says calmly, "you have been in a serious car accident. You have undergone a four-hour surgery. I placed a titanium rod in your femur. You have five incisions, two by your knee and three by your hip, as well as abrasions to your face and chest. Now is not the time to be a hero."

I look from Mom to Mimi to the doctor. No one speaks.

There is a whole conversation going on in their silence, but I'm not invited.

"Eight. I'm an eight," Mom says with all the cheer drained out of her.

"Right," Dr. Lipman says. "I'll put an order in to up your morphine dose."

Her *what*?

Mom closes her eyes.

"Morphine." The word is a lit match. It sets all my trust on fire. How *could* they? I look to Mimi for help. Mimi is the Mom whisperer. She'll throw out an AA quote and the doctor will get it and Mom will just have to deal with the pain, because *that's what people do*. They deal with it.

But Mimi doesn't do that. She nods at the doctor instead, like she was hoping for this all along! For the first time since I have known her, I hate her a little.

"We can give you a pump if you like," Dr. Lipman suggests, "with a button you can push as needed so you can regulate your own pain."

"No!" Mom says, her voice cracking. "No pump. I don't want to be in charge. I'll leave it to the professionals." She laughs weakly. I bite my tongue so I won't yell, because you can't yell in a hospital unless you're dying. Right now it feels like I am.

Mom's eyes drift shut as the doctor starts to explain to Mimi more about the tests they're running tomorrow. It's clear Mom's done for today. So am I. I move toward the door. No one notices. I make fists with both hands to stop them from shaking.

A few seconds after I walk out I hear Mimi huffing behind me to catch up. I do not slow down. When we get in the elevator, I leave a wide space between us. If she says *one word* to me, I will hit the stop button on this elevator and let her know *exactly* what I think of her and this whole situation. *You don't do this to a person after three years of building trust. You don't give drugs to the* drug addict*!*

But Mimi stays quiet, so I say the rest in my head. *You're a liar. Just like Mom.*

6

GRANT ME SERENITY

I END UP EATING the last of the Hamburger Helper cold, standing in front of our fridge, just so I can cross it off the list. And also, to be alone.

I place the Tupperware in the sink and watch the bubbles lift up the crusted edges of old cheese and oily crumbles of meat. A hard scrubbing and it'll be good as new. I wish people worked like that. I grab the bristled sponge and attack the container even though it hasn't soaked long enough and the water is too hot.

As Mom's sponsor, Mimi should know better. It took Mimi *twenty years* to get sober. It sounds like a prison sentence, because it is one. The addiction locks you up until you figure a way to break out. Except it's not just the one person serving time—it's anyone who ever cared about them. I thought Mom and I had put in our time, but it's not black-and-white like that.

I remember the early recoveries, big celebrations for three days, six weeks, three months sober, when Mom would make a cake from scratch and blow out a candle but let me make the wish. At first I wished for real things—a Little Mermaid helmet for my scooter or a Rubik's Cube. Then after a while I'd just wish for this time to be different. But it never was—until we moved here. I thought.

I sit on our beat-up green couch that we got at Goodwill and christened Oscar because of his mossy color and fuzzy Muppet-ness. The plastic bag of Mom's belongings from the hospital lies on the coffee table screaming at me to open it. Honestly, what right does she have to privacy? As Mimi always says, we're only as sick as our secrets.

I pull the bag into my lap and begin setting everything out on the table like a crime scene investigation.

Item #1: Crocheted hedgehog key chain with keys to our van, which is currently sitting in a tow lot across town.

Item #2: Five cinnamon-flavored Jolly Ranchers— the reason Mom smells like Red Hots everywhere she goes.

Item #3: Pink glittery wallet filled with a driver's license, three crumpled dollar bills, and a Starbucks gift card from a cleaning client who

thought that would   nicer Christmas gift than
cash. We don't nee   puccinos. We need to
pay our bills.

Item #4: A Cherry   Smacker, which Mom
took from me and   take back.

Item #5: Mom's o   cracked, but not from
the wreck. It was   way. I hold down
the power butto   happens.

I walk into my bedroo   lug the phone into the
charger. Which is in my room   she never remembers
to do it.

Back in the living room,   everything else in the
bag and glance at our sunshi   on the wall. It's 8:12
p.m. I don't have to check my   know what happens
in the laundromat every Wedn   t at eight.

I creep down the stairs, skipping the creaky third step
from the bottom, and peek through the small round window
in the door. I don't even have to put my ear to the wood to
listen. These walls are thin enough that I can hear everything.

The orange chairs that I swept under this morning are
now arranged in a circle in the middle of the room. The
sign has been flipped to CLOSED. That's two nights in a
row we've shut down early. This town is small enough for

everybody to know the reason why Mimi's becomes a different kind of space on Wednesday evenings. Three grown-ups sit with an empty chair between each of them, like they don't want to get too close. They're all looking at Mimi. The air smells like burnt coffee and powdered sugar from the box of Entenmann's donuts on the table. We are right on schedule.

"Hello. As you all know, my name is Mimi and I'm an alcoholic. Welcome to the Cedarville group of Alcoholics and Narcotics Anonymous," she says. Looking at her in her worn-out overalls and Birkenstocks with socks, you'd never know she was an aider and abettor. Right now Mom is lying in her hospital bed with that IV drip, drip, dripping drugs into her veins. I huff and my breath fogs up the glass.

"Let's open this meeting with a moment of silence for the addict who still suffers," Mimi adds, and they bow their heads, all except one, Derek, the youngest in the group. He's college aged without the college part. He works over at the Oil Express. He's so skinny, his jeans fall in folds like a skirt.

It's a small, familiar group, but Mimi always begins the same way. First snacks, then the moment of silence, then the Serenity Prayer. Then she reminds everyone there can be no drugs or alcohol on the premises. Only after all that does she open the group up for sharing. That's when it gets good.

"Would anyone like to start?" she asks. Silence. Chairs squeak as people shift. It's like the call for prayer requests at church on the rare occasions we go. No one wants to be the first to open up their own can of worms.

Mimi takes a sip of coffee and looks around, meeting everyone's eye who will let her.

"All right then, looks like I'm up to bat," she says, and leans forward so her elbows rest on her knees. "Like I said, I'm Mimi, and it'll be twenty-one years of sobriety for me this April. Despite what the songs say, drinking never made my life more fun. I lost too many good years and good friends to alcohol, and so I'm just happy to be here with you all tonight, with a business to run and people I love."

Next she's supposed to share about a moment she was tempted this week and came up victorious. Or a memory she has of when she was at her worst. That's how it's supposed to go. She stops and looks down.

"Speaking of people I love, you'll have noticed we're missing one of our regulars." She clears her throat. "Jules was in a car accident yesterday, and she's in a bad way. She's up at Memorial West with a long road to recuperation ahead of her."

Derek leans forward. "Was she high?" He's too inter-ested, too excited. But still, I scoot closer until my nose touches the window of the door.

Mrs. Lois, the one who looks like somebody's grandma and brings her knitting to the meetings, says, "Hush, boy," like he took the Lord's name in vain.

"What? It's an honest question. We're all about the truth here, right?" Derek runs a shaking hand through his hair as he names the elephant in the room. Derek is an "irregular" regular. He only shows up half the time, usually after a particularly bad round of uppers, the drugs that make you jittery and forget to eat and sleep. Mom's drugs of choice, like oxy, always made her sleepy and spaced out. I once found her lying on the kitchen floor, staring at her hands and whispering "Keep calm and carry on" over and over again. Either way, up or down, you lose.

"Derek's right. We don't keep secrets here," Mimi says. "She wasn't high." I close my eyes, but before the relief can settle in, Mimi continues. "But as you all know, it's a tricky path to walk, managing pain with a severe injury and a history of drug abuse."

"Nancy Reagan told us to just say no," Mr. Pete, one of the custodians at my school, says, and then shakes his head and coughs out a laugh. I like Mr. Pete. He smiles at me when he comes around to collect trash at lunch.

"Well, Nancy didn't break her femur yesterday," Mimi barks. Everybody freezes. She never loses her cool at these meetings. With rude customers in the laundromat, sure, but not here.

Mr. Pete holds up his hands like *I surrender*. "It was just a joke. Bad one, I guess."

Mimi sighs. "Sorry, Pete. It's . . ." She pauses. "Narcotics are designed to treat pain under a doctor's supervision. And that's where Jules is now—*in pain* and under a *doctor's* care. This isn't a relapse for her. She didn't—she *doesn't* want to take the pain medication, but you didn't see her." Mimi's voice breaks. She hunches over like someone punched her. Out in the hallway, I do too. Worry is a physical hurt.

No one speaks. That's another rule in this group—after you share, you get as much time as you want to collect yourself. When Mimi eventually sits up, she wipes her eyes with the heel of her hand.

"I have to believe that the doctors know what they're doing and that Jules is strong enough to get through this," she says, more to herself than to anyone else. "Let's say a prayer for Jules tonight, who is one of us, for healing and hope and continued recovery."

As they bow their heads, I creep back up the stairs, not bothering to skip the creaky third step.

7

BACK TO REALITY

MONDAY, MARCH 10

Leave PB&J + water + Tylenol on coffee table for
  Mom

8:15 a.m.—Meet with Ms. Taylor about makeup
  work

Math—FINALLY ask Mr. Jamison about extra
  credit

English—FINALLY turn in paper

5:00 p.m.—help Mom with PT exercises

Dinner—???

"BABY, CAN YOU PASS ME that box of thread before you leave?"
Mom calls from her spot on Oscar the Couch, which she
hasn't left since she came home. With fabric and thread
boxes and ribbons draped all around her so she can reach
them, she looks like a bird in a very colorful nest.

I dig around in her craft closet, which is the only closet
in our apartment. Our clothes are left to fend for themselves

in the jam-packed wardrobe that Mom "refurbished" with sandpaper and sunflower decals.

"The reds or the yellows?"

She doesn't glance up from the wooden embroidery hoop on her lap. "Burnt umber through russet."

I lift plastic box after plastic box until I uncover the one full of reds and carry it to the already full coffee table.

"You sure you can reach it?"

With the quilt on her lap, you can't even tell she's hurt, apart from the bruises on her face. But I helped her change the bandages last night, and there's no ignoring the three-inch incision by her hip or the four other tiny cuts where they drove the nails into her bone to keep the titanium rod in place. It sends squiggles through my stomach just to think of it.

But when we picked her up from the hospital on Friday, she pretended not to feel it at all. She waved to the nurses like a prom queen as we pushed her down the hall in her wheelchair, and when we got outside, she tilted her face up to the weak sun and smiled like she was standing on the deck of a ship. On the ride home, she sang over and over again from the back seat of Mimi's pickup truck,

"Your knee bone's connected to your thigh bone
Your thigh bone's connected to your hip bone
Your hip bone's connected to your back bone
I heeeeeeeear the word of the Looooord!"

We finally had to turn on the country station to drown her out. This is typical Mom—anything even remotely serious or sad becomes silly. She can't sing her way out of the fact that she is now vanless and unemployed. But as long as the silliness isn't from the pain meds, I can handle it. For now.

She catches me watching her as she snaps a length of thread in two with her teeth. No amount of sewing is going to make me forget that this is the first day she will be left unsupervised. As Mimi would say, you can put lipstick on a pig, but you can't make it smile. Some situations can't be prettified.

"I'm okay, Franny. Stop worrying about me." She tugs one of my brown curls. Not for the first time, I wish I'd inherited her straight blond hair. Maybe I wouldn't stand out so much at school. Then again, Mom makes all our clothes and therefore 90 percent of my wardrobe has ruffles, so maybe not.

"Here's Mimi's portable." I set the old cordless phone on the arm of the couch. "She says you can use it to call her on her cell anytime. She'll run right up."

Mom nods and shoos me toward the door, and I feel a twinge of guilt.

For the record, I *know* lying is bad. But I also know that stress is a trigger and nothing good can come from impatient Uber requests or angry messages from cleaning clients and insurance companies. So when she got home and asked where her phone was . . . I fibbed. I told her it got destroyed in the crash. Then I went to my room and buried it in my backpack, where it is now fully charged and very much in working order. Never was there a more noble lie.

I also did not tell her about the pills I hid in the kitchen drawer underneath the take-out menus. When Dr. Lipman handed her the bottle of ten oxycodone tablets, Mom said she didn't need them. But apparently, once the prescription is filled, you have to take them with you. Also, I'm not a monster. I don't *want* Mom to be in pain. If it comes to it, *I'll* be the one to decide when and how much she gets. The phone, the pills, the food in the fridge—this is all part of how I help her heal.

8

BACK-TO-SCHOOL BLUES

BACK AT SCHOOL, everything is the same, except worse. Ms. Taylor, the counselor, has decided that the teachers should give me my makeup work a little at a time so I "don't get overwhelmed," and she's also making each of my teachers assign me a "homework buddy" in every class who will be responsible for sharing their notes with me from the three and a half days of school I missed. She seems to think I'm still in kindergarten.

Ms. Taylor is also the one who handed me the laminated "How to Beat the Worries" chart after reviewing my files when I first came here. It had a bright yellow sun smiling at the top.

HOW TO BEAT THE WORRIES

1. Tell the worry to GO AWAY when it pops into your head.
2. Lock worries away in a strong box in your mind and make them wait for WORRY TIME.
3. Use LOGIC to make the worry less powerful.

4. Reset your system with ACTIVITY and/or
   RELAXATION.

These are the dumbest ideas. Telling worry to "go away" makes me picture a giant storm cloud or maybe the Nothing from *The Neverending Story*. You can yell all you want, but it doesn't listen. Also, "Worry Time"? Am I supposed to go sit in a corner and worry for five minutes and then—*bam!*—pop up good as new? Also, how do you put your thoughts in a box? Worry is like water. It leaks.

The only one that ever worked for me was using logic, because if I can understand the reason behind something, I can picture all the parts and put them together in a way that makes sense. Logic is a puzzle you get to solve. And nothing beats worry like a solid answer. For example: I will get an A in math because, statistically speaking, I always achieve the highest score in that subject. Another example: It takes twenty-one days to form a habit and it's been more than a thousand since my mother got clean, so obviously she won't relapse over these measly eight hours while I'm away from her at school.

I'm trying that last one out today. It's not quite as solid, because it requires me to ignore the five years *before* that, when she relapsed over and over again. I need Worry Point #4: Activity. Today's mantra is "Stay busy!" Which is why I'm standing outside Mr. Jamison's room early, ready to ask for that extra credit. I hitch my bag up higher on my shoulders and march in.

"Sir, I meant to ask you last week if I could take on some extra credit. Maybe something with probabilities? I like working the odds."

Mr. Jamison rubs a hand over his buzzed hair and sighs. Hmmm. This is not the reaction I expected. Mr. Jamison loves me. Even though he tries to hide it, I'm his favorite, and I'm not ashamed to admit it. You have to have *one* place you win in middle school, and math is my place. So why won't he just hand over the extra credit? Students file in behind us. I take a lesson from Mimi, look him right in the eye, and wait him out.

"Well, Franny, you know I'd love to." He stops to clear his throat. "You're one of my brightest students."

The brightest, I think, but teachers aren't allowed to say that.

"Great, so . . ." I hold out my hand, ready for the work. Confidence is everything.

"But, well, you have quite a lot of work to make up, and I know your situation at home . . . isn't easy right now." He adjusts his glasses. Ms. Taylor got to him.

My arm falls.

"Let's focus on the tasks at hand, and then we can talk about adding more, okay?" It's a question, but also not, and he at least does me the kindness of not expecting an answer. "In fact, I was just about to tell you who your homework buddy is," he continues. "I thought one of your tablemates would be the simplest choice."

He points to our table by the window, and the hairs on the back of my neck rise with that scary-movie warning. Something very bad is about to happen.

Nopleasenopleasenoplease. I pivot slowly toward my table.

"Sloan seems like a good match."

And there it is.

Sloan waves and throws Mr. Jamison one of her fake smiles. It morphs into a smug grin that makes my skin itch when I walk over. *Sloan Tate* is my tutor. Logic just flew out the window.

I sink into my seat, pull out my planner, and keep my head down. It doesn't stop Sloan from leaning over and whispering, "Nice dress," and gesturing at my yellow sweater. It would have been a perfectly fine sweater if Mom hadn't cut off the bottom and sewn giant folds of pink lace to the lower half. It's now something a seven-year-old would wear to a fairy princess party. Also, it's the total opposite of Sloan's look: all spandex, all the time. Athleisure wear at its best, just in case anyone forgets for one second that she's a cheerleader.

"Thanks."

"Whoa, got a one-syllable word out of you today! It's a whole new Frances. Looks like the time off did you good." She narrows her green eyes at me and leans in. I catch a whiff of coconut body lotion. "You don't *look* sick. Why were you *really* gone?"

All the muscles in my stomach tighten. The granola bar

I had for breakfast starts crawling back up. This is why I don't talk at school. No one else bugs me like Sloan. Most people just ignore me because I ignore them. It's not that I don't like people. It's just that my schedule is full. I don't have time for small talk. But when I got an A on our first official math test of middle school back in August and Sloan didn't, she decided I was her target. Cheerleader versus Nerd. It's so clichéd. I'd tell her that. But that would require talking to her, which I try not to do at all costs.

Before I can stop her, she grabs my purple planner.

"No!" I whisper.

She holds the planner out of reach. "Let's just check the record to see what's on the old agenda." Her thin lips stretch into a smirk. She can't see my planner. She's going to know that I make Mom's lunch and that I help Mimi count change and that I cook dinner most nights and hide in the library when I can't stand eating in the cafeteria. My whole *life* is in there. My nose begins to tingle in that about-to-sneeze-or-burst-into-tears way. If Sloan sees me cry, it will end me.

Behind us Lacey and Rosa stop staring at their phones under the table and lean forward, trying to figure out what's going on. In ten seconds this will turn into something big enough to whisper about in the hall. Or worse.

"No," I beg. "Please."

"Cut it out, Sloan." A long-fingered hand reaches around me and plucks my planner from her. It's a miracle.

44

"Here, Franny," Noah says, returning it to me. I just barely stop myself from hugging it like a blanket. Noah is the only other person at our table, but we have never spoken, apart from group work.

"Thanks," I mumble, and tuck my planner back in my bag, where Sloan will never get her hands on it again.

Sloan rolls her eyes at Noah. "Well, aren't you the knight in shining high-tops."

He ignores her. I steal a glance at him over Sloan's head. I've never paid much attention to Noah Lee before. He's never given me a reason to. As a starting basketball player, he's up there with Sloan as one of the kids people hover around. This school is basketball crazy. It loves basketball like Texas loves football. I've never been to a game, but I don't need to—I can get the play-by-play all day long, from eight thirty in the morning until dismissal at three twenty-five.

Noah leans over his math book, folding something, his fingers moving quickly, like Mom's do when she's sewing. I let myself wonder, for just a second, what his deal is outside this place. He's never stepped in to rescue me from Sloan before. Why is today different? It's not like I'm in his circle. I have no circle. I am a dot.

"How's the studying going?" Sloan asks, and I blush because she caught me looking at him. She glances from me to Noah, who is oblivious, and raises her eyebrows. Then she elbows me in the ribs for no reason. Sloan is one of those hands-on people. She bumps into your shoulder, pokes you, pulls at your bag when it's on your back. It's like having an annoying little brother for an archnemesis.

"Mr. Jamison said you had notes for me," I say to change the subject.

Surprisingly, she gives them up. I'm about to say thank you, out of a politeness reflex, until I open her notebook. These are not notes. These are doodles of flowers and dogs and ten-sided stars with one equation in the middle that isn't even done correctly.

She sees me scrunching my nose at it.

"What?"

I'm saved from an answer by Mr. Jamison returning the quizzes we took last Tuesday in class, the *first* half, before my world flipped upside down.

He's not one of those teachers who makes a big deal of passing papers back facedown so no one can see each other's grades. So when he hands the quizzes back one at a time, first to Noah, then to Sloan, then to me, I check them all: 89, 98, 96. "Good job, table five," Mr. Jamison adds before moving on to the next group.

Sloan got two points *better* than me? She catches me looking and sneers.

"Why don't you go ahead and keep those notes. I don't need them anymore," she says, and whips her ponytail in a way that only a cheerleader can.

9

DON'T PANIC

I HIDE IN THE BATHROOM during lunch and call Mom.

"Baby! What are you doing calling in the middle of the day? Are you okay?"

I wince from my spot in the last stall. I forgot I don't technically have access to a phone. I count the blue cinder-blocks on the wall. Six, seven, eight. Thank goodness Mimi's portable phone doesn't have caller ID.

"Yeah, uh, I'm okay. I'm calling from the office," I say finally. That's lie number two. Or is it two and three? "I wanted to check on you, make sure you took the Tylenol I left. There's another dose laid out on the table for three p.m."

I can hear the familiar *scritch* of our old record player switching over. Mom works best with noise. Her most frequent Uber comments are from customers praising her Spotify playlists.

"Franny, I got it. I ate the sandwich, took the pills, and managed to get myself to the bathroom without tripping on my embroidery hoop! Ha! How's that?"

I close my eyes. She sounds all right. No slurring. No long pauses before she answers. I tell myself, *again*, that we're okay. Twenty-one days to make a habit. We're over a thousand. She's good. We're still good.

"I even made three of my cross-stitch quotes for the Etsy business today," she adds.

In her spare time, Mom stitches goofy sayings onto small circles of fabric and sells them on Etsy. They're nothing fancy, but people seem to love them. Everything's funnier in cross-stitch, I guess.

"How's this for a zinger? 'When life shuts a door . . . open it again, that's how doors work.'" She chuckles. "It's covered in purple wisteria vines with a tiny door at the bottom."

"Nice one, Mom."

"Oh, there was something else. . . ." She trails off and I hear her snap her fingers. "Wait! I wrote a note to myself so I wouldn't forget it." Paper rustling. A loud thud. She must have dropped the phone. Then she's back. "Got it! Can you do me a favor since my phone's lost, along with all my contacts?"

I hold the "lost" phone to my ear and swallow. In our living room, Paul Simon sings about Graceland and Mom waits for me to answer. She always makes sure you say yes before telling you what you're agreeing to. It's what led to our brief mobile pet-grooming business. It ended in disaster when a cat named Barthole*meow* clawed his way up the back seats and escaped through the sunroof.

"Uh, sure."

"Excellent. My regular cleaning clients are probably wondering where I disappeared to, but since it took me fifteen minutes to get myself to the toilet, I don't think I'll be down on my knees cleaning theirs anytime soon. I need to let them know. You're the organized one. Didn't you keep a backup list of their numbers somewhere?"

Her regulars—the people she cleans for each week who pay us enough to offer Mimi a tiny rent and put food on the table. What are we going to do without that money? Worry fills my stomach like a balloon, until it's tight and stretched and I have to bend over in the stall. Her Etsy projects are fun, but they don't pay the bills. Uber was unreliable at best. Now we don't have that, either.

"I have them written in my planner," I say with my head between my knees. "I'll call them for you from Mimi's phone if you want."

"Thanks, kiddo! See you at four, right?"

"Uh, it'll be later tonight. I'm staying to make up work. I'll catch the late bus home." Lie number . . . whatever.

"'Kay. Kisses, Fran." She makes a loud smacking sound into the phone and hangs up. I lean my head against the wall and take a deep breath, in for four and out for four, like the counselor made me practice back in Memphis.

After ten rounds of this, I come out of the stall and hit the button I've been avoiding on Mom's phone: voice mail.

The first three are from Mrs. Ivey. She's the oldest of Mom's regulars, both in age and how long Mom's been cleaning for her—since the very first month we moved here. She's also the only one whose house Mom cleans twice a week. "Julia, dear, are you okay?" she asks at the end of each message in a wobbly voice. The last one is eight minutes and seventeen seconds long because she forgot to hang up.

The Ellsworths didn't call, but Mrs. Ellsworth sent several texts, demanding to know why Mom hadn't shown. They have by far the biggest house and pay the most, which I guess in Mrs. Ellsworth's mind means she can treat Mom however she likes. Her last text reads, *If you do not respond ASAP, we are more than happy to find services elsewhere.* Mom missed *one* cleaning session. Sheesh.

The Kusels, the young couple who run the new gourmet grilled cheese place in town, didn't call or text, thank goodness, but it's only a matter of time.

I'm about to put the phone away and head to lunch, where I will pretend to eat because my nervous stomach is still chewing on this morning's granola bar, when a number I don't recognize flashes on the screen. I panic and send it straight to voice mail. And then I wait. And then I listen to the message.

"Hello, Ms. Bishop. I hope you are well. This is Meredith from the billing department at Memorial West. Please give me a call at your earliest convenience so we can discuss a payment plan for your recent hospital visit. Thank you and—"

I smash the power button before she finishes. *Not ... enough ... air.* The room gets dark, darker. Water. I need water. Out of the stall, face in the sink, I gulp straight from the tap. The whooshing is soothing. The blackness leaves. I look at myself in the mirror. My hair is a wild tangle. A damp line runs along the bottom of my sweater from leaning against the sink.

I haven't had a panic attack in years.

Weak and shaky, I walk back to the cafeteria and sit at my usual table next to the trash cans, which smell like wet hamburger. I don't even pretend to eat.

We're not going to make it. What happens if we can't pay the hospital bill? Will they sue us? Will we have to leave Mimi's? The only other option is Memphis, and that's not an option at all.

I am staring at my tuna sandwich like it might hold the answers when a piece of paper flicks across my table. I pick it up. It's a bird—a tiny bird made out of paper.

"The wings aren't even, but it's as close as I can get with regular notebook paper."

I look up. Noah is standing in front of me with his hands in his pockets. He steps closer, his neon-yellow Nikes brighter than the surface of the sun. I open my mouth, but nothing comes out. I offer up the bird. He must have dropped it by mistake.

His hands stay in his pockets. "Nah. You keep it. I've got hundreds."

"But . . ." That's the best I can do. The bird tips in my hand. We stare at it. My brain is glitching. Too many things have happened in the last hour and a half.

Questions I'd never ask in real life start running through my head. *Why did you decide to start talking to me all of a sudden? How did you learn to make this? Do you give them to everyone?* I don't really want to hear the answer to that last one, because it's probably yes and he is just a boy who is bored.

"You seemed quiet in math. Quieter than usual," he explains, like he read my mind. Spooky.

"Quieter than usual," I repeat. What's my usual amount of quiet?

Out of the corner of my eye, I see Sloan leaning back from her regular cheerleader-filled table to watch us.

"Well . . . thanks?" I say, and he nods and walks away like it's no big deal. I look at the bird. Noah is a big scribble in my brain I can't work out. So I set the bird down and pull out my planner instead.

In the back are blank pages for notes. I press the lever on my pen with black ink—the color for serious thinking. Then I begin to fill the page.

10

CLEANLINESS IS NEXT TO GODLINESS

TEN MINUTES LATER, I BITE the tip of my pen and study my new "Monster Money List." Then I think something I would *never* admit out loud: *sometimes math isn't fun.*

MONSTER MONEY LIST

Money going out

Physical Therapy: $75 per visit X twice a week for twelve weeks = $1,800

Hospital Bill: $$$$ Thousands??? (Does other driver have to pay? RESEARCH.)

Van: Status unknown. Bus fare: $65 for 31-day pass

Rent: Whatever we can manage, because Mimi never asks

Groceries: $50 a week or less (shop ONLY on double coupon day)

Money coming in

Mom's Etsy cross-stitch: $30–40 dollars per
piece depending on size X 8 pieces per week (if
we're lucky) = $240 to $320 (per week) = $960
to $1,280 (per month)

~~Cleaning Clients: 4 visits @ $90=$360 (per
week)=$1,440 (per month)~~

~~Uber: Highly variable, depending on airport
traffic and tips. Estimate $800 (per month)~~

Mom can say we'll be fine all she wants. But there's one thing I know for sure: numbers don't lie. Without money from her regular clients, there's no way we'll make it. We can't *afford* to cancel.

I move the paper bird closer to me for comfort. There's only one solution. It's risky; a one-in-a-million-bazillion chance of it working. But if I can pull it off, it will be the best idea of my entire life.

Very carefully, I cross out helping Mom with PT on today's agenda and write something new.

Mom is getting paid today, whether she knows it or not.

The smell of sweat mixed with gasoline and the vibrating of the bus engine makes me a little sick. I watch the trees pass and hug my backpack. The plan I came up with at lunch is in motion.

I get off at the back of the bus so I don't have to speak to the driver. As I walk up the small hill toward the Royal Oaks neighborhood, I get a flicker of fear. No one knows where I am. *It's for the greater good,* I tell myself, and press 1919* to get into the gated community. Today at four I will clean a house, collect the money, and begin to pay the debts we owe. It's a long shot, I know. All the houses, all by myself, without getting caught. But the clients won't notice or care who cleans as long as they return to a home that smells like lemon, right? Also, there's still schoolwork to catch up on and Mom to take care of, but I can't think about that now. Clean first. Think later.

The wind whips the ends of my purple coat back and forth like a kite as I get closer to the Ellsworths' house, which is so big it has a separate house for all their cars. What you can't see from the street is the third house in the backyard, a playhouse version of the main house they built for their daughters when they were small. I ate lunch in it every week last summer. It has windows that open and rocking chairs on the porch.

I knock and hold my breath. The arrangement has always been that the clients are out while Mom cleans, all but Mrs. Ivey, who doesn't ever leave. But this is not the Ellsworths' regularly scheduled time.

Silence. *Whew.* I key in the code to unlock the door and enter when it clicks. The place is cavernous. It's literally like a big hollow cave that echoes when you walk or accidentally drop your backpack, which I do. It hits the hardwood with a *thwap*.

I grab the cash first. It's tucked next to a note Mrs. Ellsworth left on the kitchen counter: *Please change sheets in master bedroom.* I only have two hours to mop, sweep, polish, dust, and Clorox the living daylights out of this place. And it has to be perfect, because it has to look like a job done by Mom.

No one who had to actually clean their own house would design it this way. The creamy yellow hardwood floors show every scuff and must be mopped and then rubbed with an oily solution that won't come off your hands no matter how many times you wash. The master bedroom, kitchen, and outside porches all have their own fireplaces with mantels to polish and stone hearths to sweep with a wire brush. The fridge is one of those stainless steel giants that shows every fingerprint and requires a special spray. Lucky for me, Mrs. Ellsworth never cooks, so the stove and oven stay clean. Unlucky for me, the two daughters, now teenagers, use the microwave in the downstairs kitchen like it's an Easy-Bake Oven. It's forever coated in crusty macaroni and fizzled hot fudge sauce. The sink smells like alphabet soup.

I get to work.

One hour and forty-three minutes later, I am scrubbing black mold out of the cracks of the second shower downstairs and nowhere near done. My puny arm muscles burn—too much math, not enough push-ups. I've got a bleach spot on my sweater. I knocked over the open trash bag in the kitchen *after* I mopped, which means I have to do it again. There's no way I'm going to finish.

I scramble out of the tub, out of the room, and all the way out the patio doors, until I am standing on the deck with my head hanging over the rail. I pull off my rubber gloves and throw them into the bushes.

That's it. I quit.

II

UNWELCOME GUESTS

THE YELLOW RUBBER GLOVES HANG from the rosebushes like a big neon sign that reads SOMEONE WAS HERE AND UP TO NO GOOD!

I slink down the stairs and fish them out, pricking my finger on a thorn in the process. The sting of it startles me back to the present. Right. I need to get out of here and never come back. The plan was a huge fail. *But* I can totally quit and nobody has to know. Except . . . I've never quit anything in my life. And if I quit, there's not even a *minuscule* chance we can pay our bills.

I turn and look up at the ginormous house and remember something Mom said to me when she tried to teach me to cross-stitch. It was supposed to be a ladybug, but I crissed where I should have crossed, so it looked more like a radioactive spider. I got mad and threw it across the room. She made me pick it up and keep going. "Not everything has to be perfect. Sometimes, kiddo," she said, "good enough is good enough."

Right. I can do this. It's not going to be perfect, but it's going to get done. After a couple of deep breaths I head back up the stairs and finish the job like someone is chasing me. I rinse the shower one last time, squirt bleach gel around the rims of the toilets until the water is a deeply reassuring blue, then race up the stairs, throw the dirty sheets into the washing machine, and hit start. On my way out I rearrange the family photos just enough on the bookshelf in the living room to make it look like I dusted all the way to the back. Then I race away ninety dollars richer.

The chilly night blows away the smell of disinfectant, and my bad mood. I run down the hill. It wasn't perfect, but I did it! Now all I have to do is move everyone's cleaning time to after school, tell Mom I'm staying late for the math extra credit that I am *sure* Mr. Jamison will give me once I get caught up, and then sneak the money into my super-secret BILLS jar I keep stashed behind the cereal bowls in the kitchen. It's my emergency fund, in case something happens and the puny amount in our bank account runs out. Now Mom can focus on getting better and we can all get back to normal as soon as possible.

Back at home I burst through the door . . . and into a crowd.

There are more people in our apartment than I have ever seen. Mom sits on Oscar. Meg, the physical therapist, is packing up a large black duffel bag. Mimi leans against the kitchen counter with her arms crossed and a fierce scowl on her face. Two women I kind of recognize as church ladies from Cedarville Presbyterian stand halfway between Mom and Mimi in the space that is not quite kitchen but also not quite living room. They're the ones getting Mimi's death glare.

No one is speaking.

Either something went down right before I arrived, or it's about to. The room is thick with unsaid things. But looking at Mom, you wouldn't know it.

"Hi, kiddo!" she calls cheerfully from Oscar. I inch my way past the two women and toward her. Her smile is bright, but her eyes are tired. Eyes don't lie. She has that barely hanging-on look. My heart double-beats. Did her stitches open? Did she fall? I look to Meg, the medical professional. She hands Mom a stapled packet. It's covered in blurry black-and-white pictures of legs bent in various positions. It's strange to see all those limbs on the page without bodies attached.

"Thursday, same time," Meg says, in a voice surprisingly deep for someone so small. How can we trust she knows what she's doing? What if she's working Mom too hard or in the wrong ways? Did Mom even *ask* about her work experience? Maybe since we have no money, they gave us a dud.

"Thank you, Meg," Mom says. "Oh, and here!" She presses a bright violet scarf into her hand—not sensing the possible dud-ness of this woman at all.

"Thank you?" Meg stares at the scarf like she's not sure what it's for. Eventually she places it in her Nike bag and makes her way to the door. Mom is always doing things like this—giving away her work for free to people who don't or won't appreciate it. *This* is exactly why I started the BILLS jar.

"Sorry about that, just finishing up," Mom says to the two ladies hovering by the door as Meg shuts it behind her. I sit on the arm of the couch and Mom puts a hand on my back. It feels good. My muscles are tight from all the scrubbing and lies.

"You don't apologize to them, Jules," Mimi grumbles. "Your home, your schedule."

"So nice to see you already on the mend!" one of the ladies chirps, ignoring Mimi. Wow. *Nobody* ignores Mimi. But this lady, with hair so red it has to be from a bottle, seems like a spitfire too.

"Well, thank you," Mom replies, ever polite, just like she taught me to be, even though it looks like all she wants to do is go to bed. "This is my daughter, Frances." I wave.

Mimi frowns so deep, her lips disappear. She pushes away from the counter. "And how did *you* come to know she needed mending, Ruthann?" She circles like a guard dog and sits on the other side of Mom.

"My daughter works at Memorial West," the second woman, who introduces herself as Barbara, says. Her voice is softer. She wears one of those flowy outfits you see on old ladies—like a bunch of handkerchiefs layered on top of each other. She seems nice enough, but Mimi tsks.

Ruthann steps forward and Barbara takes a tiny step back.

"Carl sent you, didn't he?" Mimi's knee bounces up and down, and Mom puts a gentle hand on it. I've never seen Mimi so worked up. It's awesome.

"No, Naomi. *Pastor* Carl didn't send us. This is just something the ladies of the church like to do. We bring meals"— she holds up a casserole dish—"to those in need."

"Well, that's awfully nice," Mom interjects before Mimi can get in another word. "I'd stand, but . . ." She laughs lightly in that way that puts people at ease, and Ruthann and Barbara smile.

"Oh, don't worry, honey. We'll leave this on the counter, and there's a salad and some of Barbara's cranberry squares. Those'll need to be refrigerated."

Ruthann opens the fridge and begins to shuffle things around to make room. "Well, make yourself at home," Mimi mutters.

When the food is successfully put away, Mimi herds the church ladies to the door.

"We'll keep you in our prayers, Julia," Ruthann calls from the doorway. "It was nice catching up, Naomi. Maybe we'll see you Sunday at church?"

"Oh, I expect not. I'm running a business, and we are

open seven days a week." She steps between them. "Clothes need cleaning as well as souls. Me and God have our own system worked out, thank you. You can tell *that* to Pastor Carl."

Ruthann twists her mouth like she's trying to figure out if this is blasphemy or not.

Mimi puts her palm against the back of the open door. "I am taking *this* opportunity to accept the things I cannot change and change the things I can. Good night." She shuts the door right on Ruthann's nose.

"That seemed uncalled for," Mom says, straight-faced. She's dying to laugh. It's good. She looks less tired than a few minutes ago.

"Did you just quote the Serenity Prayer at them?" I ask to keep the happy moment going.

"Darn right, I did, Franny, my girl," Mimi says, and grins.

All the tension left the room along with our visitors, and my stomach knows it. It comes out of hiding and growls. I walk over to the kitchen counter and lift the foil off the casserole. Creamy chicken covered in buttery crackers and poppy seeds. Perfection.

"Well, *I'm* not sorry for the visit," I say.

Mimi rolls her eyes.

"What's with you and the pastor?" Mom asks, removing the blue bandana from her hair to use as a makeshift napkin when I hand her a plate.

"Me and *Carl* have a history. That's all I'll say," Mimi says, carrying over water glasses.

I raise my eyebrows at Mom. We love it when Mimi gets worked up.

While they're busy making space on the coffee table for our dinner, I turn my back on them in the kitchen and ease open the menu drawer. The small orange bottle of oxycodone is exactly where I left it. I roll it to the side so I can see past the label and count out ten. Good. All present and accounted for. I breathe out slowly and close my eyes for a second in sweet relief. Mom is doing okay. We're about to eat a home-cooked meal that none of us had to cook. And tonight, after Mom is asleep, I'll slip my earnings into the BILLS jar. Things are right on track.

12

PUBLIC HUMILIATION

WEDNESDAY, MARCH 12

Get Mimi to heat up chicken casserole and
administer Tylenol

Math—give Sloan her (terrible) notes back

Take #10 bus to Mrs. Ivey's

Buy extra rubber gloves and more of Mom's
hand cream (green jar)

"WHAT'S WITH YOU?" SLOAN WHISPERS as I pass back her math notes without a word.

"Nothing."

"Why do you keep scratching like that?" She pokes my arm with her pencil, like I'm something she found on the bottom of her shoe.

Something in the Kusels' all-natural cleaner has given me a rash. I can't stop rubbing my arms.

"I'm not."

"You *are.*"

"I'm *not*."

"Ladies," Mr. Jamison says. "If you've got so much to say, why don't you come up to the board and finish this equation."

Sloan and I groan. For once we're in agreement.

Noah whistles and claps. "Go, table five! Repre*sent*!" Mr. Jamison looks startled. Math doesn't typically get cheers.

I take the marker first. It's an easy set of integer problems, and I work until Mr. Jamison tells me to pass the marker to Sloan. She won't take it. She stands there with her hands on her hips. My arm shakes from holding it out, waiting for her to make a move. What is she *doing*?

Mr. Jamison rubs a hand over his head.

"Sloan?"

"Yes, Mr. Jamison?"

"You're up."

"I'm sorry," she says, and then gives me a look that sends shivers all the way from my head to my toes. Something's coming. Something bad. I shift my feet and scratch my arm. She smiles. "Mr. Jamison," she fake-whispers so the whole room can hear, "I don't feel comfortable sharing a writing utensil with Franny. I think she might have some sort of *skin condition*."

Laughs spew like fizz all over the room before Mr. Jamison can stop them. I drop my arm. Mr. Jamison says something to Sloan about seeing her after class, but I can't really hear him over the ringing in my ears. *Get me out. Get me* out.

He sends us both to our seats, and I grab my bag and

run for the door. Noah calls, "Wait," but I don't. I run until I am in the last stall of the bathroom with the door locked. I count the blue cinder blocks until I can breathe again and the panicky darkness goes away. When it's over, I am clammy and so much more tired.

I hide in there until the bell rings. The bathroom fills and empties again. I hear Lacey at one point. She's telling the whole thing to Aliyah from my science class. I catch snatches of it: "rash or something" and "needs to take a bath" and "it's just so sad." I plug my ears after that. When I am alone again, I splash cold water on my face, dry my hands, and pull out my planner to review the rest of the day.

One benefit of cleaning is that you can't think about much else while you're doing it. I follow the lines the vacuum makes across Mrs. Ivey's shaggy carpet and let my mind go blank. Up. Down. Up. Down. Hit the corner. Turn around. Her house is an easy clean. Nothing ever moves, and she seems to only eat canned soup and Lean Cuisines, even though part of Mom's job is to buy her groceries every Friday.

The work is simple, but the fact that Mrs. Ivey is *around* for it is not. She's eighty-three and never leaves the house. Mostly she sits in the recliner in her bedroom or out on the back patio with her white poodle.

I stand up and stretch from where I've been wiping down the baseboards with a damp rag. I start to scratch my arm and force myself to stop. The rash is already going down. It stings less than Sloan's words.

That's what teachers get wrong. They think it's one big thing that makes someone a target for meanness. But it's not. It's a thousand small things, like a random rash or weird clothes or being too quiet or too serious or too slow with the comebacks. It's owning a purple planner and actually using it. It's having a mom who cleans houses instead of owning one. It's being good at math but bad at people.

I shake my head and get back to work.

"Where'd you say your mama is?" Mrs. Ivey yells from the one sunny spot on the patio where there's a break in the pine trees that grow along her back fence. Her crown of white hair sways like a dandelion in the breeze.

"She's helping Mimi with her remodel, Mrs. Ivey!" I've had to invent a renovation project to explain why I'm here and Mom's not. I like lying to her even less than I like lying to Mom. It seems meaner when you lie to old people.

"That laundromat has been there twenty years! You tell Naomi, if it ain't broke, don't fix it!" she shouts. Petunia, her poodle, shivers in agreement.

"I'll be sure and tell her."

"What?!"

"I'll tell her, Mrs. Ivey!" I holler toward the open door. She looks smaller than the last time I saw her, but maybe it's just her pink dressing gown. It drapes over her shoulders like a coat on a hanger. She doesn't look warm enough to be outdoors. But it's not my business.

After giving the kitchen counter one last wipe, I take the money and the grocery list from where they're stuck to the refrigerator with a magnet of a giant tooth that reads SNODGRASS DENTAL.

"I'll be back on Friday with your food!"

"And your *mama*, right?"

I make a noise that isn't quite yes or no and gather my backpack from next to the front door. I look back at Mrs. Ivey, sitting alone in the breeze, talking to her dog. On Friday I'll bring her one of those puzzles she likes from the newspaper—the ones with the fill-in-the-blank sentences.

"Bye, Mrs. Ivey!" I call.

"Don't forget to get the soft stuff for Petunia! Even if it's not on sale!"

"Will do!" I shout, but I don't think she hears me. She's bent over Petunia, mumbling something about *everybody always in a hurry*.

When I slam the apartment door after getting home from Mrs. Ivey's, something is off. I don't know what it is at first until I scan the living room and the kitchen: no Mom. My hands start to tingle, and it's not from the rash. *Don't panic, Franny*, I think, and call out for Mom. When she doesn't answer, the tingling spreads to my arms.

13

C IS FOR "COMMUNICATION"

"MOM! *MOM!*" I SHOUT, higher and higher pitched. Still no answer. I drop my bag and run down the narrow hall toward her bedroom, my heart thumping as if I'm being hunted.

I stop short at the half-open bathroom door.

There's Mom's elbow resting on the edge of the tub. I thump my forehead on the doorjamb. Of course she's having a lovely bath while I've been at school hiding in a bathroom stall and scooping Petunia's poop out of Mrs. Ivey's yard. I sigh. Guess this means I'm doing my job of keeping her from getting stressed.

"I'm home," I say into the crack of open space.

Nothing. Why isn't she answering? I put my hand on the door, but I can't make myself push it open. The tingling is back.

If this is another Before and After, as in "*before* I know the very bad thing and then *after*," I want to stay in the Before.

The After finds me anyway. . . .

• • • •

I was four and playing in my room with the doctor's kit Mom found at a yard sale. It had laminated charts of the human skeleton and a vision test and little pill bottles you could label with a dry-erase marker. It had been six months since Mom slipped on our apartment steps and hurt her back. We were in and out of doctors' offices so much, I became obsessed with all things medical.

I was playing in my room, because that was where Mom told me to go. She said she had to study. Before the accident she never told me to go to my room. It was always the two of us, side by side. I was trying to read the "Doctor's Checklist" and listen to my own heartbeat with the toy stethoscope. After a while, I noticed the music in the living room had stopped. Mom always studied with music. I figured if the music was over, she had finished, and I could go out and sit with her.

The living room had that bubbly popcorn stuff on the ceiling. I loved to climb on the couch and pick it off when no one was looking. The one lamp in the corner never managed to stretch its light more than halfway across the room.

It wasn't the best apartment, but it was all we could afford. Mom had taken out loans to pay for college. But she could never finish, because she had to work full-time to pay for the loans that paid for the school and also take care of me.

"Mom?" I whispered, because I could see the back of the couch, but I couldn't see *her*.

"Mom?" I called, louder.

I don't know how long I stood there—kind of like the way I'm standing here now, outside the bathroom door—before I walked all the way in. It was long enough for the exact placement of the couch and lamp and table and television to imprint itself onto my brain.

I saw her foot first, jutting out from under the coffee table. She was on her stomach with a bottle of pills next to her. I screamed. She didn't move. I got down on my hands and knees and shoved her. It was like pushing a bag of sand.

I'll help her! I thought, and ran back toward my room to get my medical kit. But I tripped on the leg of the coffee table on my way there and slammed my chin into its edge. My teeth crunched together with a sound like tires on gravel. I couldn't see for a second. My mouth filled with blood. I let it drip while I cried. I found Mom's phone wedged between the cushions of the couch. But I didn't know who to call. Mom had made me pinky-promise never to call 911. She said, "Pals like us don't rat each other out." I didn't want to be a rat, but I didn't know what else to do. So I hit Home in her contacts and my grandma Jean answered. I'd only met my grandparents a few times.

By the time they got there, with coats thrown over their pajamas, Mom had woken up. We were sitting next to each other on the couch. I was biting down on a washcloth to stop the bleeding, and Mom was crying into her hands. I wanted to tell her "it's okay" and "I'm sorry I'm a rat," but I was afraid to take the washcloth out. I was afraid of the blood.

We moved in with my grandparents that night.

No, this can't *be that. Not again. Please,* I beg the universe, and push open the bathroom door. Mom's head rests on the back of the pink clawfoot tub, not moving.

"Moooom!" I moan.

I reach her in two steps and raise my hand. I slap her once as hard as I dare. She gasps and screams, and I fall to my knees. Water rushes over the edge of the tub, drenching my jeans, and I don't care because she's alive. This is not the worst After.

"Franny?" she shouts, ripping the headphones off her ears. "What in the *world*?"

Her right cheek is bright red from my slap. I can make out the individual shapes of my fingers.

"Sorry! I'm sorry!" I stop and gulp air. Every part of me prickles with that pins-and-needles feeling.

"Honey, *what*?" she asks, her hair dripping over us both as she reaches for me. She smells like roses—her bubble bath.

"You didn't *answer* me. I was calling and calling and you didn't answer!"

"I couldn't hear you!" She points to the headphones and her relic of a CD player. I kick it, and it cracks against the wall in a way that doesn't sound fixable.

Silence fills the room and spills out the door. I am not sorry about the CD player.

"Help me out of here." She points to her leg, which is wrapped in plastic and draped over the side of the tub. "It took me half an hour to get myself in."

I'm still mad, but I hold out my arms so she can grab on and pull herself up. Once she's out, she wraps herself in her old silk robe. By the time we hobble into the living room and collapse on Oscar, the anger is gone and I've started crying. I can't make myself let go of her. She rubs my back in smaller and smaller circles and waits it out. After a minute, or maybe an hour, I wipe my nose on the shoulder of her robe and whisper, "I didn't know where you were."

"Where would I be?" she says, tugging at the end of my hair and smiling. *Smiling.*

"Dead in a ditch!" I shout, because how dare she smile.

"Franny—" She tightens the tie on her robe and puts her hands on my shoulders. I stare at a bald spot on Oscar's cushion.

"This is my fault. I should never have left you alone. I'll take a break from school, help out around here until you can move better. I can teach myself. I bet I'd do better than half my teachers. I—"

"*Franny.*" She traps my fluttering hands in hers. "Look at me."

"No."

"*Look. At. Me.* Good. Now breathe in for four."

I shake my head, but then she starts and I can't stop myself. It's impossible to watch someone breathe like that without doing it too, like yawning.

"Okay, hold."

She holds her hand up for a count of four.

"Now out for four," she says. We deflate together.

I feel better, which makes me feel worse. I overreacted. When the universe kept her safe after the car accident, I made a promise that I would trust her. Now I've broken it. You shouldn't make deals with the universe you can't keep.

Whatever Mom sees on my face must make her think the breathing trick wasn't enough. "I want you to say the first three *C*s with me."

I blame Mimi for this. She taught the *C*s to Mom, who decided they should become the "Franny mantra." There are seven *C*s in Narcotics Anonymous; they're for kids whose parents are drug addicts. *They* do drugs and *we* get homework.

"Mom, no."

"The first three. Come on." She lets go of my hands and leans back on Oscar. "And then we'll have brinner."

Breakfast for dinner, "brinner," is my favorite thing. She knows this.

"*Fine.* One: I didn't *cause* it." ("It" being Mom's addiction to all her substances of choice.) "Two: I can't *cure* it."

"And three?" she asks.

"I can't *control* it." I roll my eyes, because I *can* control that. I don't agree with the *C*s. But I'm not telling Mom that. *Why* can't I cure it? Whoever came up with the *C*s never met me *or* my mom. They don't know our situation. It's like randomly picking a Band-Aid out of the box and hoping it's the right size.

"Now say the last four for me."

"You said brinner if I did the first three."

She tucks my hair behind my ears. It doesn't stay.

"Humor me."

"Okay, but I want pancakes." I pick up where I left off and say the last four really fast. "I can't control it, but I can *care* for myself by *communicating* my feelings, making healthy *choices*, and *celebrating* myself."

When she hugs me, her wet hair sticks to my cheek. "Let me worry about me, baby girl," she whispers in my ear. "I promise to take care of myself if you promise to do the same."

"I would like to take care of myself with pancakes and blueberry syrup now," I say. She laughs, but I'm still rattling around like a lost coin.

14

FLUKES

MOM THINKS I'M DOING my math extra credit after brinner, but
I've snuck down the stairs to watch Mimi call the Wednesday
AA meeting to order. Mom, in a sundress covered in daisies,
sits with her freshly bandaged leg stretched across three
orange chairs. Her hair is still damp from the bath. Derek
and Mr. Pete basically had to carry her down the stairs.

Mimi dumps a package of Chips Ahoy on a plate and
passes it around. "All right, folks, you know the drill. Welcome to the Cedarville group of Alcoholics and Narcotics
Anonymous. I'm Mimi, and I'm an alcoholic."

"Hi, Mimi!" Mom waves like she's meeting her favorite celeb in real life. Mr. Pete and Mrs. Lois chuckle. Derek
crosses his arms over his skinny chest and ignores her.

"Why, hello, Jules. Welcome back," Mimi says, pretending she didn't just see her five minutes ago upstairs. "Would
you like to start?"

Mom's hyper from too much brinner coffee and her first
real social interaction in a week. Her good leg bounces to a

silent beat. She's not great at being alone. It's why she can't clean a house or drive a car without music blaring to keep her company.

"Sure, I'll start, unless Derek would like to jump in." She bumps shoulders with him, and Derek blushes all the way to his bleached hair before he remembers he's angry at the world.

"No? Okay. Well, folks, as you can see I got pretty banged up last week." Mom taps her leg with a half-eaten cookie. "It was the first time I've been in the hospital since, well—" She glances at the door I'm currently hiding behind, and I duck. I'm not supposed to be here right now. No kids in meetings. Hence the "Anonymous" part of Alcoholics and Narcotics Anonymous. What's said in the meeting stays in the meeting, or between you and your sponsor. Those are the rules set by God or whoever invented AA.

But I figure I've earned the right to know how Mom's *really* doing when all she'll tell me is she's "fine" and "don't worry." I've been eavesdropping since we showed up three years ago with a van full of dirty laundry and Mom fresh out of rehab. Mimi says that addicts can always recognize other addicts. It must be true. She invited Mom to her first meeting that night.

When I hear Mom talking again, I lift my head and watch.

"—since I OD'd one thousand, one hundred, and sixty-four days ago. But who's counting?" She laughs, but she's the only one. She brushes crumbs from her dress. "Anyway, I'm still clean, and I am proud of that." She tilts her chin up. "I can handle the pain."

"But?" Mimi prompts. She isn't Mom's sponsor for nothing.

"Buuuuut," Mom says, dragging it out, "it's the stillness that's getting to me. I'm used to go-go-going, you know?"

She leans forward and puts her hands on her knees and then winces. I want to yell *Stop moving like that or you'll pull your stitches!* But I stay quiet and hidden.

"I miss my routine. I miss Molly at the fabric store. I miss playing Justin Bieber too loud in the van."

"You can listen to the Biebs anywhere," Derek says, sounding so genuinely confused that a tiny laugh bubbles up, and I cover my mouth.

"I know," Mom says, patting his knee, which turns his entire face crimson. "But I miss Ubering and making small talk with the out-of-towners catching rides from the airport." She sighs. "I miss climbing up onto the roof with Franny and watching the stars."

My heart wobbles. I miss that too. It's a tradition we started on our fire escape in Memphis. The muggy air smelled waxy orange from the citronella candle that was supposed to keep the bugs away but never did. We have a few raggedy lawn chairs up on the roof, and when it's nice, we have night picnics: tea and crackers and bits of leftovers and music until the sun goes down. It's awesome.

I stare at her banged-up leg and her wrinkled dress. It'll be a long while before we have another rooftop picnic.

Back in Memphis I'd sit tucked in her lap, listening to the crickets chirp and watching the stars twinkle. She would say I was the Little Dipper to her Big Dipper—Little D and Big D, the dynamic duo. That was before the slip on the stairs. Before that first prescription for painkillers. Before we moved in with my grandparents. Before she dropped out of community college. Before all the rehab centers.

Before.

What if she'd just gripped the handrail on those stairs a little harder and *hadn't* fallen? Would she have finished school? Would we still be in Memphis? Would I have friends? What a stupid fluke to ruin a life.

"Fluke"—that's what I heard my dad call me once when Mom accidentally put him on speaker in the car. He's in Idaho or Iowa or Indiana. One of those *I* states. I can't remember. I try *not* to remember. They met in college, but when they found out they were having me her freshman year, he couldn't handle it. She won't tell me exactly what went down, only that he "had a five-year plan and it didn't involve being a dad." She doesn't seem too broken up about it. When people talk about their parents, I can't even imagine it— having a *pair* of people who think they know better than you.

I met him once. When Mom was in one of her rehabs, he picked me up after school and took me for ice cream. A double scoop of mint chocolate chip. He asked if I liked science. I said yes, and he smiled and handed me a napkin without really looking at me. He had a wife and a job fixing computers in the I state. A regular kind of life, no flukes included.

"What I'm asking," Mom says now, "is how do I stay busy enough to keep myself from thinking about using when I can't *move*?" She doesn't *sound* like the mom who just fixed me dinner and said everything was going to be okay. I get that sick feeling again, like I'm a fish and someone's tipping my bowl.

Mrs. Lois drops her knitting in her lap. "Oh, honey. There isn't enough busy in the world to keep you from thinking about it. But that doesn't mean you have to do it."

Mr. Pete stares down into his coffee cup. Derek pops each one of his knuckles. *Crack. Crack. Crack.* It sounds painful.

"Lois is right," Mimi says. "Thoughts aren't actions, and actions are what counts."

Mom nods, but it's the kind of thing you do when you just want somebody to stop talking. You don't believe it. Not really.

15

SLOW AND STEADY

THURSDAY, MARCH 13

Avoid Mom

Avoid Sloan

Avoid all humans if possible

THERE IS SOMETHING GREEN on my seat in math. I approach it with caution. It could be a Sloan trap. She got three days of after-school detention for what she said to me in class, and she is *not* happy about it.

But when I get to my table, I see that the green thing is not a trap. It's a turtle made out of green paper. The paper is thin and waxy and so light, I can't even feel it in my hand. It has a tail. I forgot turtles had tails.

"You like him?"

I jerk and the turtle drops onto the floor. Noah picks it up. So much for avoiding all humans.

Noah hands it back to me. "So, you like him?" he asks again.

"Who?"

He points at the turtle. Oh, right. *Him*, the turtle.

"I do."

"Well, good." Noah takes his seat, legs out, elbows propped on the back of his chair, like he's home in his living room. I don't understand people who can be comfortable anywhere. I'm barely comfortable on Oscar the Couch. My mind's too busy zipping around. I sneak another look at him while he's unpacking his bag. His laces are untied. Who forgets to tie their shoes?

"Why'd you give me this?" I ask.

He opens his mouth, but Sloan edges her way between us before he can answer. "Ex*cuse* me." She shoves my shoulder with hers, which was completely unnecessary because I was already scooting back. I sigh inside and move the turtle to the farthest edge of our table, where she can't squash it like a bug.

The rest of class is boring in a good way. Sloan takes notes that are mostly doodles of trees and vines and Angry Birds and pretends I don't exist. Afterward, I take my time packing up to let her go first. She does, in a rush, but not before yelling behind her to Lacey and Rosa, "No, I can't meet up after school. I have *detention*," and shooting me a dirty look.

I sigh for real when she leaves.

"Turtles are winners," Noah says into the open space between us now that Sloan is gone. He hasn't even begun to put away his books and notes.

I look at my little turtle with his tail and head in the air like a dog. "They are?"

"Yeah. Slow and steady. They're never in a hurry, but they *always* get where they're going." He nods at the turtle on the table.

"Unless they get flattened on the highway." I realize too late that is not a normal thing to say. This is why I don't talk to people.

Noah busts out laughing. It's a big huge laugh that comes straight from the gut. "Turtle pancake! Scrambled turtle!"

"Turtle toast!" I shout, and we both crack up. I can't remember the last time I laughed for real in front of someone who wasn't my mother or Mimi.

Jeremy, another guy on the basketball team, stops at our table and catches me grinning at Noah before pointedly looking past me to him. "You up for some pickup after school?" His not-looking reminds me of what Noah's attention made me forget for a second: I am invisible. And I like it that way, at least when it comes to guys like Jeremy.

"Nah, man. The season just ended. I need a basketball *break*. Besides," Noah adds, "I got work after school."

Jeremy picks up the turtle. I want to snatch it back out of his big sweaty fingers, but I am trying to be invisible, so I pin my hands between my knees instead.

He tosses it back onto the table, its tail now bent. Noah doesn't react.

"You're the only sixth grader I know who thinks he needs to *work*, man."

Noah picks up the turtle and begins to smooth it out. I would never be that chill if someone was bugging me like that. How does Noah do it?

"Whatever, man," Jeremy says finally, and shoves Noah's head, but it's playful. "Saturday, though—you and me at the courts on Del Rio?" He leaves without waiting for an answer.

"I gave you the turtle," Noah says, like Jeremy never happened, "'cause I thought you could use some cheering up."

Oh, right. I grab my bag. He's being nice because he feels sorry for me. The kid who Sloan humiliated in front of the entire class. The turtle pancake.

"Well, I *don't*. Take it back."

"Are you serious?" He looks around like someone is pranking him.

I shove the turtle toward him. "One hundred percent." Those odds should be pretty easy to figure.

He holds up his hands, won't touch the turtle. I'm about to let it fall to the floor and walk out, because I don't *need* a pity gift, when Mr. Jamison calls my name.

"Franny, can we speak for a moment?"

"Yes, sir."

I grab my things *and* the turtle and walk to his desk. Noah shuffles past. I don't check to see if he looks back at me.

Mr. Jamison smiles and holds out a blue folder. I take it

and open it, my hands operating on instinct while my mind still tosses Noah's words around like dice. Why does he think it's his job all of a sudden to cheer me up? Why is my problem his problem? Then I finally register what I'm looking at: advanced integers, variables, positive and negative numbers, probabilities, and some stuff on graphs I've never even seen before.

"Extra credit," he says, and taps the folder. "You've earned it. You made up all the work you missed and then some."

I don't know what to say. I hug the folder to my chest. It's the most beautiful thing I've ever seen.

"You have a gift, Franny." Mr. Jamison's eyes crinkle at the corners behind his glasses.

"Thank you," I whisper.

"And I'm pretty sure you'd find a way to sneak in extra credit anyway," he says with a laugh. "I might as well help you along." Too true.

I walk out the door, turtle in one hand and blue folder in the other. Noah was wrong. I don't need cheering up. I need a *challenge*—to make me forget Sloan and the pills in the kitchen drawer and the half-empty BILLS jar. I tuck the turtle into my bag and keep walking.

16

IT WORKS IF YOU WORK IT

TODAY IS MY FIRST "DAY OFF" since taking on Mom's cleaning business. She never cleans on Thursdays. I'm tempted to stay late at school and get a head start on the blue folder, but I pack it up along with my turtle and take my regular bus home instead. I haven't helped Mimi count change or refill the vending machines in a week.

A mom with twins in a stroller sits by the window staring at her phone while her toddler thumps each washing machine with an Iron Man action figure. A man sleeps in the corner with a newspaper in his lap and his head back against the wall. It's a pretty slow afternoon.

Wait . . . that man looks familiar—gray goatee, ball cap, khaki cargo pants. I know him. He's the old man from the bus—my *other* bus! He's the one with the yappy dog who rides the same route every Monday and Wednesday.

I abandon my coin-counting plan and dart up the stairs, heart thumping. Of all the ways to get caught. Yappy-dog man will not take me down. I'm already replanning the next hour in my head when I open the apartment door. I'll change into a T-shirt Mom *hasn't* bedazzled and grab a snack. With my new fitness routine (aka cleaning), I'm always hungry.

I'm making a beeline for the fridge when, behind me, Mom lets out a sharp yelp of pain. I whirl around, heart in my throat. She's lying on her side on the couch. Meg, the PT, stands behind her with her hands on Mom's knee, which is lifted at an angle I haven't seen since Mom went through a yoga phase two summers ago.

Meg counts, ". . . three, four . . . ," and pulls Mom's knee back farther, "and five, six . . . Remember to breathe."

Mom cries out again. Her breath comes fast and shallow, and her face glows bright red. Beads of sweat dot her forehead, and her blue bandana is damp along her hairline. She gives me a half wave and tries to smile, but it turns into a grimace. Meg is *hurting* her.

"Stop," I say to Meg. Meg doesn't stop. She keeps counting. "Seven, eight . . . okay, one last big breath . . ."

A tear leaks out the corner of Mom's eye. That's it. I dart around the couch and yank Meg's hands off Mom's leg.

"STOP," I order, and grip Meg's arm harder than necessary before letting go. She steps back, unfazed. I hate everything about her—her neat black ponytail, her half-zipped workout top that reminds me of Sloan, her stupid black Nike bag, Mom's violet scarf tied to the handle.

"Franny!" Mom exclaims—still out of breath, I might add—"I *asked* Meg to push me a little farther today."

"Why?"

"Because," she says, taking her bandana off and using it to wipe her face. "The quicker I can get full use of my leg, the sooner I can get back to my life. 'It works if you work it,'" she says with a wink, quoting another AA saying, courtesy of Mimi. "Plus, there's only so much needlepoint a woman can do before she goes a little crazy." She reaches for something on the coffee table. "See?" She laughs, but it's not the gut-busting good kind of laugh I had with Noah earlier. She holds up a piece of fabric covered entirely with black stitches. On top of that, she's sewn one single word in huge white letters: "NOPE." That's it—a black hole with "NOPE" in the middle.

"I dig it," Meg says, and leans closer for a better look. I glare at her.

"Consider it a well-earned tip," Mom says, and hands it to Meg. That's thirty or forty bucks we could have made on Etsy! I huff loud enough for Mom to raise her eyebrows at me, but Meg either doesn't notice or doesn't care. She takes the fabric gently before handing Mom a bottle of water, tightening her ponytail, and packing up her bag.

"Franny, please show our guest out," Mom says, and I know this is her way of telling me to be nice, so I follow Meg to the door.

"See you Monday, Julia. And remember to hydrate!" Meg calls out before turning to leave.

Then, when we're both on the landing and out of ear-shot, she says, "I know you're worried about your mom, but she's tougher than she looks." She nods toward the open door. "She did good work today." Then she claps me on the shoulder like we're old pals and leaves.

I watch Mom through the open doorway. Her hand shakes as she lifts the bottle of water to her lips. I really wish people would stop telling me not to worry.

17

POSSIBILITIES

FRIDAY, MARCH 14

Leave toast next to Mom's crutch so she has to
  use it

Math: Probability test! Ask Mr. Jamison if I can
  switch tables

Finish extra-credit integers during lunch (in
  library)

Add to Mrs. Ivey's grocery list:
  —Breath freshener bones for Petunia
  —Nonslip bathmat for shower

I GET A LITTLE BLOOD on my blue folder—I can't help it. The corners of my thumbs won't stop bleeding where the skin has split. It turns out nothing can protect your hands from the wire bristles of a fireplace brush, or bleach that slips inside your gloves when you're rinsing out a bathtub, or the bits of food stuck to a microwave door you have to pick off with your fingernail. People are gross.

My hands look crusty. If Sloan sees them, I might as well just spend the rest of the school year in the bathroom. When Mr. Jamison begins passing out our tests, I tug down the sleeves of my hoodie. Thankfully, Sloan seems too busy cramming at the last minute to notice. She's flipping the pages of her notes so fast, there's no way she's actually reading them.

I glance over her head at Noah. He's drumming a rhythm on the table with his fingers and does not look at me. We're back to normal. He can get on with his life as super-chill sports guy, and I can get on with mine as . . . whatever I am. Still, my heart gives a sad squeeze. The bird and the turtle sit on my windowsill at home. I can't make myself throw them away.

"Please use a blank sheet of paper as a cover sheet, and remember to show all your work," Mr. Jamison says as he passes our table. "No calculators, people. I want to see each step of the process."

He checks the clock on the wall. "You have forty-three minutes. Good luck and Godspeed!" He salutes us and sits at his desk.

I skim the test. After the work in the blue folder, this is easy. I haven't gotten as far through the extra credit as I'd like, though. I'm so tired after school and cleaning and helping Mom with her exercises that I don't have much brain power for anything past heating up dinner and collapsing into bed. I've been napping in a corner of the library during lunch.

Still, *these* problems I know how to do. I pick up my number two pencil and begin. Twenty-one minutes later I am done and checking over my work when I hear a *click, click*ing sound on my right. I pause to listen better, but the sound stops. I wait a moment or two. Nothing. I must have imagined it. I start reviewing my test again.

Click. Click. Click-click.

I pretend to keep checking, trailing my pencil down the page, but I sneak a peek. Sloan has her calculator in her lap, and she's using it to *cheat on our test*. She glances sideways and catches me watching. Her eyes go wide with panic and then narrow again. I keep looking. She keeps looking. We are locked in a death glare, and for *once* I'm not going to be the one to break. Five, six, seven seconds tick by before she caves and turns her shoulder to me.

The clicking resumes. It's a dare. She doesn't think I'm brave enough to tell on her. She's right. But it's not because I'm chicken. It's because I already have enough trouble. I don't need to borrow hers. I pull my cover sheet back over my work and place my hands in my lap. Then I sit there for the next twenty-two minutes, until the bell rings and Mr. Jamison collects our tests.

Sloan corners me in the hall before lunch. I cringe when she grabs my elbow and pulls me to the side by the water fountain. I was really looking forward to a nice nap.

"You didn't see what you think you saw," she hisses.

"*Oooooo*kay," I say, and pull my elbow from her grip.

"I mean it. I was checking back over my work. That's all."

It's such a bad lie, I have to shut my eyes to keep them from rolling.

"I have special permission!" she says, twisting her pony-tail in both hands. "My learning specialist wrote a note!"

I'm *sure*.

When I still don't say anything, she cries, "You don't have proof!"

I cross my arms.

"So if Mr. Jamison asked you to retake the test in front of him, you'd be able to do it without the calculator?"

She puts her hands on her hips. Her red Adidas jacket matches the red Nike swoosh on her shirt. My hoodie has a plaid ruffle sewn to the bottom, but I'm still not backing down.

We stare at each other as other kids pass, laughing and oblivious, on their way to lunch.

"Fine," she sighs, and then squints at me suspiciously. "What are you going to do?"

Up until now, I hadn't thought of *doing* anything. I am a firm believer in staying out of other people's business so they'll stay out of mine. But for once I have the upper hand. I have ... power. Do I tell Mr. Jamison? Sloan would fail the test, for sure, and maybe even get suspended. Basketball season just ended, so she's not cheering right now, but if they find out, they might not let her come back when the next season starts. I think of Sloan poking me, shoving my bag out of reach, teasing me for my clothes, accusing me of having a skin condition and *humiliating* me in front of the entire class. If anyone deserves to get caught, it's Sloan. But can I really do it?

"I don't know yet."

She takes a step closer.

"You don't *know* yet? What's that supposed to mean?"

You can only push a person so far before they push back. I move toward her so our faces are inches from each other.

"It *means* I need to think about it." I hold up my planner, which I've been holding in a death grip. "I'll get back to you, ohhhhh"—I pretend to flip through it—"let's say Monday."

"You're kidding me, right?"

"Do I look like a kidder?"

She gives me a once-over, letting her eyes drift from my hoodie ruffle all the way down to the sequins Mom hot-glued to my sneakers. I dare her to say *one* thing. But she doesn't.

"See ya Monday," I say, and push past her toward the library to get on with my nap.

18

THE BENEFITS OF TOGETHERNESS

I DON'T SEE MIMI out in the dirt on her hands and knees in front of the laundromat until I almost trip over one of the black plastic flower cartons spread all over the sidewalk. I was too busy replaying my conversation/confrontation/ *collision* with Sloan. Now she expects me to give her some sort of answer on Monday, and I have no idea what I'm going to do. This is why I should just keep my head down and my mouth shut.

Mimi squints up at me from under her faded green John Deere cap. "Late again tonight."

"Yeah, math group."

"Mm-hmmm."

I shift back and forth, studying the cracks in the sidewalk. I've told her about the math extra credit and the "study group" a million times. She still asks me where I've been every afternoon. I start to sweat in my hoodie.

"Well, now you can help me with these vincas." She gestures at the purple flowers lying on their sides looking kinda wilty in the grass. "After working your brain all day, it'll do you good to use your hands."

If only she knew how much my hands could use a break right now. The skin on my knuckles cracks open again as I slip on a pair of gardening gloves and get down on my knees in the dirt. I've got to keep pushing. The BILLS jar isn't nearly as full as I need it to be. I started to sort it but got so depressed I shoved it all back in without counting it.

"Here, you've got to break up the roots a little after they've been in the carton. Let 'em breathe. Like this." Mimi cups the bottom of one of the flowers and gently wriggles the square of dirt that holds the roots together until it comes apart. I pick one up and do the same.

We work in silence—freeing the roots from their squares and planting them in the flower boxes that hang over the edges of the big front windows. Compared to scrubbing toilets, this is easy work. I feel my shoulders relax as we get into a rhythm.

"So," Mimi says after a while, "how's school going?"

I freeze, one hand buried in the roots of a vinca.

"It's good."

I do not tell her about Sloan. Or Noah. Or the fact that when I got out of bed too fast this morning, black spots swarmed across my vision like bees. I had to hold on to the dresser until they went away. All the cleaning is wearing me out.

I change the subject to a worse one. I don't want to talk about this, but I can't ask Mom.

"Is the van totaled?"

Mimi nods and keeps working while my whole world falls apart again. I drop my flower. I wonder how long Mimi's known. I bet all the dollars I don't have that she's known since day one and didn't tell me because she didn't want me to worry. I could clean a million houses and I'd never have enough to buy us a car. The van, bills for the hospital and PT, groceries—it's too much. All my work to save money will be gone before it has a chance to add up. I sit back on the grass.

My face must be doing something awful, because Mimi abandons the flowers and pulls me to her. I'm half sitting in her lap, and she's got her sinewy arms wrapped tight around me. We're covered in dirt and grass stains. She's not normally a hugger and neither am I, but I don't pull back.

"We don't have the money," I whisper into her shoulder. It feels like spilling a big secret, except if anyone knows the state of our finances, it's Mimi.

"You know," she says, "people tell you you're not supposed to plant anything until after tax day in April. It's one of those general rules the world somehow decided we're all supposed to follow." She picks up the flower I dropped. "But you know what I say? If the flower's the right kind of flower, it'll be tough enough to survive."

I sniff. "How do you know what kind of flower you are?"

She sits back and looks at me. "Well, you're still here, aren't you? And so's your mama and so am I. We're a tough lot."

I don't feel tough. I feel like a brisk wind is all it'll take to scatter me to bits.

She hugs me harder right as I start to pull away. "You hear me now. We have a saying in AA—'one day at a time'— and that's all we've got, Frances Bishop, *this* day and *this* time." She waves her hands toward the almost-finished flowers and the sky turning orangey-pink from the setting sun.

"Let tomorrow worry about itself, my girl."

She says it like it's easy—like I want to get myself all in a tangle about this. No one *chooses* to worry. Worry just is. She places the last flower in its spot in the window box and stands up to survey our work. I stay on the ground.

"Right at this moment, your responsibility is to be twelve and to go inside and wash up. Tonight, we will dine on a possibly decent pot of my vegetable soup. We're all in this together, honey—you, me, and your mama. None of us has to fight this alone."

She holds out a hand to help me to my feet. "Here's another AA saying for you: 'together we can.'"

"Together we can *what?*" I ask.

She smirks and resettles her hat on her head.

"Do whatever needs doing."

I'm tired of slogans that don't mean anything when you hold them up to the light. I want answers. I take the stairs up to the apartment extra slow, noticing all the sore spots in my shoulders and hands and feet. Partway up, I half sit, half collapse. I could be using all this time to work on the blue folder instead, something for *me*. Math is my happy place. Maybe if I could clean faster, it'd be worth it. But last time I checked, I can't clone myself, so what's the point? Sitting on this step in the dark stairwell, I want to quit.

Mimi's words buzz around my head like gnats. I try to swat them away, but they come right back, so I let them buzz for a while, like you do when you know there's no escape. One thing she has right: we *are* tough. Mimi broke out of twenty years of addiction, and Mom made a whole life for us after she got clean, and I stood up to Sloan today, *really* stood up to her. Flowers get stronger when they have to fight for it. They use the elements around them to thrive. Maybe Sloan is exactly the evil, weedy challenge I was missing. "Together we can," right?

19

A LITTLE BLACKMAIL
GOES A LONG WAY

SLOAN'S EYES DART BACK AND FORTH over my shoulder. She's checking to see if Lacey or any of her other cheerleading friends can see us talking. I know she is. It's early Monday. School won't start for another half hour, so there aren't many people, friends or otherwise, to see us.

I did what I said I would. I gave it the weekend and thought over what I was going to do about her cheating. I didn't need the weekend. The idea that started in the stairwell on Friday night came back to me Saturday morning when I woke up, stretched in bed, and felt an ache so deep my bones shook. I can't keep going like I am or I'll need to steal Mom's crutch to get up and down the steps. By Sunday, as I stared at another full week of school and cleaning in my planner, I was convinced that my plan could really work. Because, well, it *has* to.

But now, with Sloan actually standing in front of me

with that scowl on her face, I wonder if I should have considered the likeability factor in this "togetherness" scheme.

"Make it quick," Sloan orders, back to her old mean self.

"Don't boss me."

"I'm not—"

"You *are*." We don't have time to argue, but this won't work if she thinks she can make me do whatever she wants.

"*Fine*. Okay." She tightens her ponytail with one swift tug. "Tell me what you're going to do . . . *please*." It's a sarcastic "please," but it's the best I'm going to get. I take a deep breath to push down all the fluttery worries over this possibly terrible idea and begin.

"Here's the deal—I have an after-school job and I need some help."

Sloan raises her eyebrows but says nothing. I start talking faster.

"I won't tell Mr. Jamison about you cheating if you come help me on this job. It's every day but Thursday, but I can do Fridays on my own. So Monday through Wednesday, after school, you'll work with me?" My voice goes up on the last sentence, which is not ideal. It sounds like I'm asking when I'm supposed to be demanding.

Sloan shakes her head, like she's trying to clear water out of her ears. "You want *me* to help you do *your* job?"

I nod once, firmly, fighting the urge to say "never mind" and back away.

She crosses her arms. "What's the job?"

Here's where it gets sticky.

"Cleaning houses."

Her eyebrows shoot back up. I'm risking her telling the whole world that Franny Bishop is basically a maid. She has plenty of ammunition already, but this would be icing on the huge, sequin-covered, Franny-is-a-weirdo cake.

"You want me to *clean houses* with *you*?"

I'm not sure which part of that sentence is more surprising for her—that she'll have to clean or that she'll have to do it with me.

"Yes. Monday through Wednesday." The key to successful blackmail is to sound definite and never forget that you have the upper hand. I mean, I have a secret that Sloan doesn't want to get out. I know she cheats. That's got to be worth a few rounds of Cloroxing and Windexing.

"No."

"No?" I'm too shocked to keep my voice down. It bounces off the walls toward the open front doors, where people are starting to arrive.

Sloan whispers, "Yeah, *no.* I'm not doing that. No way."

She tightens her arms across her chest, and it's like she's squeezing all the breath out of me.

"But . . ."

"But nothing. I am not scrubbing floors for anyone, especially not you."

Behind us, the hall begins to fill with the usual morning sounds—laughter, opening and slamming lockers, squeaking shoes. I don't have a plan B. I thought this would work. Sloan starts to walk away. There's nothing I can do. I slump forward at the exact moment she brushes past me, and her shoulder hits mine, hard.

Who am I kidding? My whole plan was a long shot anyway. Now I have to watch it disappear because *Sloan* can't be bothered to buff a mirror. The hallway blurs with tears, but before they can fall, the *Jaws* theme song booms from Sloan's back pocket. She pulls out her phone and backs up against the wall again. I blink and the world clears.

"*What?*" she growls into the phone. I'm still right next to her, so I can pick up some of what comes next.

". . . grounded this weekend . . . I can't be having you . . ."

"Mom!" Sloan shouts so loud, I jump. "That's not fair! Put Dad on the phone. He'd never—" She turns her back to me, so I can't tell what her mom says next, but I do know that she's still talking when Sloan hangs up. *That* doesn't seem like a good strategy to get out of a grounding. Sloan spins back toward me. I stare at a spot on the wall just above her left ear, because I don't know where to look.

"Right, so when do we start?" she asks.

Say what, now? "You're going to help me?" I look away from the wall and into her eyes to make sure she's not joking. They are dead cold and furious after that call with her mom.

The rest of the student population swarms around us. The warning bell rings. We're going to be late, but Sloan and I are in our own vortex now, and I can't walk away until I know how this ends.

"No," she says. "This isn't me doing you a *favor*. I'm going to clean the stupid houses so you don't get me in more trouble than I'm already in, *and* I'm only doing it for three weeks because every punishment has an end." Sloan leans so close I can smell her wintergreen toothpaste. "You swear if I do this, you'll never tell Jamison about the test?"

"I swear," I squeak.

"And what am I supposed to say to my parents when they ask what I'm doing after school? They already won't let me go anywhere fun, and they *definitely* won't believe I'm with you."

"Say you're in a math extra-credit group." The answer comes easy. I've said it so many times, it feels like the truth. "We start today, after school," I add, before she can change her mind.

She leans back and smiles. It's terrifying. "So *devious*. I'm impressed." Then she starts to walk away, but not before adding one more parting shot: "Remember, Franny, this isn't about helping *you*. I'm helping *myself*."

The bus ride that afternoon is predictable. Sloan complains about everything—the constant stopping and starting, the smell of gasoline, the slightly sticky floorboards, the itchy seats, and the other passengers, who, she whispers too loudly, "need a lesson in personal hygiene."

By the time we get off at the bottom of the hill that leads up to the Ellsworths' house, I'm wondering if I can fire her. Can you fire someone you're not paying? Because this isn't worth it if I have to put up with her prissy attitude the whole time. I will do it on my own even if my fingers fall off.

She walks right up to the big iron gates at the entrance to Royal Oaks and punches in the code.

"How did you know that?"

She gives me a smug look as the gate swings open. "This is my neighborhood."

I stop. Birds chirp in giant magnolias on professionally mowed lawns. *Of course* Sloan lives here. We could have just taken the school bus.

She waits for me, one hand on the hip of her yoga pants. If she is expecting a reaction, I won't give her one. I walk ahead to lead the way and don't say a single word until we reach the Ellsworths' front door.

I hold my hand over the keypad as I type in the code so she can't see, and she rolls her eyes. Then we're standing in the hallway off the Ellsworths' kitchen and there's nothing left to do but begin. I pull the cleaning supplies out of the closet, line everything up along the wall, and take a step back.

"The blue one is for the windows."

"I *know* what Windex is, Franny."

"Okay, but you also have to remember to use these rags." I hold up a bin of folded white towels. "Paper towels leave streaks, and Mrs. Ellsworth *will* notice."

Sloan nods, but I can tell she's already not listening. I persevere.

"This green round container is bleach powder, and it goes in the kitchen sink and all the showers. Run some water first and then dump in a bunch, more than you think you'll need, and let it soak while we do the bedrooms and the fireplaces."

I hold the Comet out to her. She opens the pantry door instead and grabs a box of sandwich cookies from Trader Joe's. Then she opens it, takes two, and pops one in her mouth.

"What are you doing?!" I yank the box away from her and place it back in the pantry, trying to remember if the nutrition label was facing out or not.

"Sorry," she says, spitting crumbs over the floor that *I* will have to mop up. She holds out the other cookie toward me. "Want one?"

"Sloan." I pause and take a breath. "You can't eat their food. Or look through their things. Or watch their TV. Or play with their dog."

She looks around. "They have a dog?"

"No, but if they *did*, you couldn't play with it."

"Why not? It's not like we're friends with these people."

"Exactly! This is a job—one they are paying us to do."

"How much do we get?" she asks, spotting the cash that Mrs. Ellsworth has left on the counter, along with a note that reads *Sweep downstairs terrace.*

I grab the money before she does. "*I* am getting paid ninety dollars."

"Ninety bucks! That's not fair! I'm doing half the work. I should get half the cash!" The New Balance sneakers she's wearing probably cost more than this paycheck, and I bet her parents bought them for her on a day that wasn't even her birthday or Christmas. She has no idea how much this money means to me. I grit my teeth. *I am a tough flower. I am a tough flower.*

"First of all"—I hold up a finger—"you haven't done any work so far." I hold up another. "And second, let's not forget why you're here." I don't bring up the test. I don't have to. It hangs in the air between us like a bad smell.

"Franny," Sloan says, wiping her hands on her pants and spilling more crumbs on the hardwood floor. "This is why you have no friends."

She picks up the Comet and walks away.

20

THE BUDDY SYSTEM

IT TURNS OUT MY CALCULATIONS were wrong. It didn't take half the time to clean with Sloan's help. It took much, *much* longer.

I had to stop *my* work to remind her to scrub the grout with the toothbrush and not the regular sponge, and I had to go *back* over the work she'd already done because she didn't vacuum in straight lines and she forgot to clean the top of the microwave. Not only did it take twice as long, but by the time we finished, I was twice as exhausted.

So when I see her already in her seat in math class on Tuesday, I am ready to tell her she doesn't have to come with me to the Kusels' that afternoon. She'll be relieved. Neither of us enjoyed my having to teach her the most basic fundamentals of cleaning. I mean, who doesn't know how to put sheets on a bed?

She elbows me when I sit down, and I brace myself for the usual comments: insults about my clothes—today my jean shorts have multicolored pockets on the back—or jokes about my hair, which is especially frizzy because I was too tired to wash it this morning.

"So, whose place are we hitting up this afternoon?" she whispers.

She looks . . . excited? It takes me a minute to understand why. And then I get it: she thinks this whole thing is a game. You can't explain "poor" to someone who's never used public transportation or shopped at Goodwill when it wasn't for a costume for theme day at school.

"Sloan," Lacey calls behind us. "Did you get number sixteen?"

Sloan holds up a hand.

"Not now, Lace. I'm *busy*."

Lacey sits back and whispers something angry-sounding to Rosa.

Never, ever has Sloan chosen to talk to me instead of anyone else except to make fun of me. It's disorienting.

I can see Noah watching us on her other side. He makes me nervous in a different way from Sloan. It's not entirely a terrible feeling. Maybe I overreacted about the turtle. I lean toward Sloan and say in a low voice so he won't hear, "It's smaller—a condo in town—for the people who own Cheesed."

"That new grilled cheese place? Their spinach artichoke melt is *amazing*!" Sloan says. One sandwich at Cheesed costs twelve dollars. Of *course* she's eaten there.

"Shhhhh," I whisper, and she manages to quiet down.

Noah looks away again, and I'm not happy about it. I should be happy about it, though. Life right now has to be narrowed down to a simple equation: add money, subtract distraction. Noah is a distraction if I ever saw one.

Sloan spends the rest of class drawing smiling grilled cheese sandwiches all over her paper, and I force myself to think of nothing but problem sets.

Before class ends, Mr. Jamison passes back the tests we took Friday. I tell myself not to look, but then I do anyway. Sloan got a 98 and I got a 95. She got three points higher than me because she *cheated*, and I can't *tell anyone* because that's the deal I made. She holds it up for Lacey and Rosa to see. Then she grins and fans herself with it. This is the person I've chained myself to for the next three weeks.

She calls, "See you after school, Fran!" and winks at me on her way out.

I put my head down on the table.

"You two are friends now?" Noah asks. I jerk my head up. I thought everyone was gone.

"What? No!"

"Seems that way to me." He shrugs, already turning away. I don't want him to.

"No." I grab hold of his sleeve. "It's just—she's doing me a favor."

He turns back. "I've never known Sloan to do *anyone* a favor."

"Well, let's just say she *owes* me a favor."

"That sounds more like it," he says.

We trade tiny smiles, until I realize I'm still holding on to his shirt and let go. My face gets so hot, I feel it in my ears. I grab my bag and move toward the door.

"Hey, Franny," he calls from behind me.

"Yeah?"

He's gathering his books but pauses. "Be careful, okay? Sloan's not the kind of person you want to mess with, you know?"

I give him a grin and a little salute, à la Mr. Jamison. "Maybe. Or maybe *I'm* the one *she* shouldn't mess with."

He laughs and shakes his head, and I'm happier than I've been in weeks.

The Kusels have left a plate of fancy cheese on the counter in the kitchen, with a note that reads:

> Hi, Julia,
> We had some leftovers at the restaurant.
> Feel free to take these home and share!
> Many thanks for all you do,
> The Kusels

And below that is a diagram of the plate, labeling all the cheeses. I would have preferred extra cash, but Sloan is all about it. She won't let me start cleaning until we try them.

"I like the Roquefort," she says, licking her fingers.

"Is that the one that stinks?"

"It's the blue cheese, top left." She points to one that looks like it's covered in mold, and I shudder. Give me Velveeta and Kraft singles any day. Part of me is glad she's here to eat it. Otherwise, I'd have to throw it away or feed it to Petunia. I can't exactly bring it home to Mom.

"So tell me, Franny," Sloan says, hopping down from the counter and stepping uncomfortably close. "How come you're cleaning houses after school? Where's your mom? I thought this was *her* gig."

Sloan might not be any good at math, but she's not stupid. I bend over and pick up the spray bottle of vinegar-and-water mixture that the Kusels like Mom to use.

"I'm just trying to pick up some extra cash," I say, almost choking on the word "extra," because when has that ever been true?

"I can respect that." She picks up the bag of folded towels and follows me into the bathroom, her ponytail swinging.

"You can?"

"Sure." She shrugs. "My parents only give me fifty bucks a month. That's barely enough to cover my music downloads. Forget about movies."

I grab the bottle and a rag and attack the sink. She gets fifty dollars for doing *nothing*? "Allowance" is just a word parents with too much money like to use so they can pretend they're teaching their kid to be responsible. I straighten to stretch my back and catch her sitting on the edge of the tub, scrolling through her phone.

Does she even know how hard cleaning really is? She knows nothing about what it takes to earn money. I emptied the BILLS jar this morning, and you know what I saw? A pile too small to spark a fire. It was never enough for what we needed, or for what we need now or might need in a month. It's never enough.

I should ignore her, do it all myself, and get out of here as fast as I can. But Noah is right. Sloan will take any opportunity to get the upper hand, and doing her job for her is letting her off the hook.

"Listen, if you don't want me to tell Mr. Jamison how you got that ninety-eight, then you have to do the work. Here." I throw the rag at her.

She drops her phone to catch it. "Hey!"

"It's clear you've never cleaned a thing in your life, so we're going to go aaaaaaaall the way back to the fundamentals, okay?"

"Wow, way to be *super* patronizing, Fran," she says, but I've got her attention. I tighten the blue bandana around my hair. Mom doesn't wear bandanas for fashion; it's the only way to keep my hair out of the bleach.

"The key to making sure you get every surface is to

picture each room like a square on a grid. Start at the top left, like here"—I point to the top of the mirror above the sink—"and work your way down and across."

I spray the mirror with Windex, and she hands me a paper towel. I shake my head and pick up a clean rag. "Never paper towels on the mirrors or windows, remember?"

"Riiiight, right." She sighs. "Do you have a rule for everything?"

"Only the things that need them," I say, and then think, *Which is everything.*

"Now, if we're still following the grid, what comes next?" I ask.

Sloan stands and looks around.

"The ugly tile by the tub?" she asks.

I shake my head.

"No. If we're cleaning everything from top left all the way to bottom right, the next step after the mirror would be the sink, then the cabinet below it. Top to bottom, left to right."

Sloan looks back and forth from the tub to the sink. A narrow line forms between her eyebrows like a crack in the dirt. Is this what she looks like when she's concentrating? How is this the *first* time I've ever seen her make this face?

"It's just like the graphs in math class." I hand her the spray bottle. "Picture it all on a grid and work through it. Get it?"

Sloan slams down the bottle of vinegar solution. I jump.

"No! I *don't* get it!"

A tremor of fear runs through me. I forgot who I was talking to. Just because she agreed to this doesn't mean she's not still the same Sloan.

I brace for impact as she moves toward me, but she sinks down on the toilet lid instead and . . . starts to cry.

I stare at her, the rag dangling from my hand. Uhhhhhh . . . this is new. I don't know what to do with a Sloan who cries. And she's really going at it—snot and tears and hiccups.

I sit down on the edge of the tub, a good foot away. If I were the type to touch, I'd put my arm around her, but I'm not, so I don't. Instead, I gently pry the bottle from her fingers so she'll stop whacking it against the floor.

Eventually she sniffs and runs her hands under her eyes. I tear off a few squares of toilet paper and hand them to her. She blows her nose.

"You know why I had to cheat on that test?"

I shake my head. I'm still not sure it's safe to speak.

"I suck at math."

I try to look surprised.

"My mom said if I want to go to gym camp this summer, I have to keep straight As."

"What's gym camp—like cheerleader school?"

Sloan groans.

"*No*, not cheerleader school. It's vaulting and bars and

the balance beam, serious stuff. I do cheerleading at school as a way to stay in shape for the tumbling team I do the rest of the year. Also, cheerleading is no joke. Have you ever thrown someone ten feet in the air and caught them by their foot?"

I shake my head and shudder. Why would anybody voluntarily throw or be thrown? She nods, dead serious. She's as intense about cheerleading as I am about math. It makes me like her more, or maybe fear her less.

"My mom doesn't get it either. She's either doing Keto or a juice cleanse, depending on whatever comment my dad made about her 'flabby arms' over dinner."

I cringe inside. Bad dads. Is it worse if they were never there or if they are? Sloan sniffs again.

"What does he think about the gym stuff?"

She shrugs. "He's a radiologist. He says anything that drives you to work hard is good." But I bet he'd draw the line at deep cleaning. He doesn't exactly sound like the manual labor type.

To prove my point, Sloan adds, "He'd still murder me if I failed math, though. I'm supposed to go to college at Vanderbilt and then med school, like him and my sister. He thinks gym is a nice hobby because, and I quote, 'a sharp body keeps a sharper mind.'"

Ick. Double cringe.

She studies her hands for a minute.

"I have cheated on every one of our math tests so far," she admits. "It's the only way I'm not failing. You talk about this bathroom like it's some 3D graph. But all I see is a sink, a toilet, and a shower with some seriously ugly green tile."

She's right. For me the world has always been like a digital version of itself—easy to break down into more manageable parts, a video game where you can zoom in on one particular thing and learn all about it and then zoom out again to see where it fits. It helps me understand *things*, but it's not much help with understanding *people*.

I look around the room and try to see it from Sloan's point of view—a toothpaste-splattered sink, a grime-circled drain, a crooked bathmat. It's a mess.

"You're right," I say after a minute, "that tile *is* ugly."

She laughs and blows her nose, then tosses her tissue into the overflowing trash can, where it falls out again. It takes everything in me not to comment.

"Listen," I say after a minute. "I'll help you with math if you want."

She frowns. "I don't need tutoring. I'm *your* homework buddy, remember?"

"Think of it like an even exchange. I help you with math and you help me clean. It can be a learn-while-we-work kind of thing."

She puts a finger to her chin like she's thinking. "Tell

you what," she says with a very Sloan look on her face. "I'll let *you* tutor me in math if you let *me* tutor you in something else."

What subject could Sloan Tate possibly know more about than me? I open my mouth to say no, but she is already tugging me out the door.

21

LESSONS AT THE DRIVE-IN

"YOU GOTTA LOOSEN UP, FRAN," Sloan says as we stare at the Sonic menu on the screen at one of the empty car slots. The smell of french-fry oil and car exhaust is making my already nervous stomach roll over. I should be home by now. How long can I say math group lasts before Mom gets suspicious? "I'm going to get an Oreo Blast and chili cheese tots," she adds. I think I might barf in my mouth.

The drive-in just off the highway sits under an orange halo of streetlights. That's how I know it's too late for me to be out. I should be home, working my way through my blue folder, helping Mom with her ninety-degree knee bend, heating up the leftover tuna casserole that Mimi made. I don't have the time for this or the money. Even the smallest size ice cream Blast is $3.39 with tax. I shove my hands in the pockets of my hoodie. "I'm not hungry."

Sloan waves her phone in front of my face. "My treat. Got the app, Fran. It's hooked up to my mom's credit card."

"So your *mom's* treat, then," I mumble, "and what are

you supposed to be teaching me in the parking lot of a Sonic?"

Sloan doesn't hear. She's too busy ordering me a large Oreo Blast with extra Oreo. And that's when I hear it over the static and the humming of car engines all around us— a familiar voice. "That'll be eighteen dollars and fifty-one cents. Thank you for your order."

I drag Sloan away from the speaker and into the grassy ditch in front of the row of parking spots. "Was that who I think it was?"

She grins her evil grin. I look past her just in time to catch a headset-wearing Noah wave through the drive-in's small set of windows. My breath hitches. *Nope. Cannot do this right now.* I turn and run through the grass toward the road, where a bus shelter sits under its own halo of light.

"Fran, wait!" Sloan shouts. I don't. But her years of leg presses and sprints work against me. She catches up in seconds and circles in front of me with her hands up like a crossing guard. "Whoa, whoa, whoa. It's Noah, not Harry Styles."

"I'd care less if it were Harry Styles!" I shout. "He doesn't sit at our math table!"

Sloan cackles so hard, she collapses on the grass in front of me. After a second she tugs my hoodie sleeve. I let myself be pulled down next to her.

"That's the point," she says. "I *know* you like him." I eye her sideways but do not confirm. "I thought you'd dig the idea of being around him outside of school—a little low-key practice with me as your buffer."

A bus trundles to the stop ahead, its brakes squealing. I could still make it. I look from it to her.

"Come on." She gets up and dusts the grass off her butt. "Order'll be up soon." The old Sloan would have taken any chance to humiliate me in front of Noah. But maybe this new version is really trying to be nice-ish.

Back at our window, Sloan pulls a wadded tissue out of her pocket and drops it in a grease spot on the ground. "Speaking of practice," she says, and bends down to snatch it before popping up with her hands held out like she's afraid of smudging her nails.

"*What* are you doing and *why* are you standing like that?"

"It's only the best move from the best movie of all time," she answers.

"That's not in *Interstellar*, last time I checked."

"That *would* be your favorite movie. It's from *Legally Blonde, obviously*. And it'll teach you the most basic flirting skills, since my guess is you have approximately zero."

She drops the tissue again. "Your turn."

"I am not touching your dirty tissue."

We are standing over the dirty tissue and arguing when a very large pair of neon sneakers appears. "Two Oreo Blasts and a chili tot." Noah. I swallow and make a grab for the ice cream for something to do with my hands. He hands me a giant spoon to match the giant ice cream, but I fumble it and it topples to the ground. Of course it does. Sloan bends at the waist and does her flip move again.

"Oh, the bend-and-snap. Nice one." Noah laughs.

I am startled out of my embarrassment enough to ask, "*You've* seen *Legally Blonde?*"

He scratches the back of his neck. "Uh, yeah. It's my moms' favorite movie. They quote it all the time." Moms, plural. Noah has two moms, makes paper animals, and works at Sonic. What else don't I know about him? "The manicurist is hilarious," he adds. And he likes rom-coms.

"She *is!*" Sloan shouts, handing me my spoon without looking at me. "We did the bend-and-snap in one of our cheer routines."

Noah chuckles. Sloan pops a tater tot into her mouth. Something unpleasant twinges in my rib cage. *She* clearly doesn't need help getting comfortable around Noah. I thought he said she was trouble. Why is he laughing with her now?

"I've never seen it." I take a too-big bite of ice cream that makes my teeth ache.

"It's about a blond girl at Harvard and a snotty brunette who is her mortal enemy until they are forced to work together and become friends." Sloan flips her blond ponytail and gives me a pointed look.

"You'd like it, I think," Noah tells me.

I open my mouth, hoping something intelligent will come out, but before it can, his headset crackles to life. "Whoops, I'm technically not supposed to be out here. I'm not old enough to serve." He looks at me. "I snuck out when I saw it was you."

I swear the ice cream in my hand actually liquefies. He jogs backward toward the building before I can say a word.

Sloan drops her empty tater tot container in the trash and clinks her Blast cup with mine. "Looks like you don't need me to tutor you in the great art of flirting after all."

I chew on a chunk of Oreo and watch Noah disappear. When it comes to that particular subject, she has *no idea* how much I don't know.

22

THE ACCIDENTAL DETECTIVE

I DID *NOT* WANT TO take Sloan with me to Mrs. Ivey's. She's a nice old lady who doesn't need to hear Sloan moan about cleaning the crusty bits out of Petunia's bowl. But Sloan *insisted*.

"I want to practice," she said. "Improve my time." She's turned cleaning houses into a competitive sport.

And of course, today is one of those rare days that Mrs. Ivey is up and about when we arrive. Sloan shakes her hand and then wipes her own on her T-shirt when Mrs. Ivey wanders into her bedroom to answer the phone. "Skin like tissue paper," she says, and I roll my eyes.

I'm passing the trash bags to Sloan when we hear Mrs. Ivey's voice through the door. "His birthday falls on Good Friday this year," she says. "I thought you could bring the kids down for Easter weekend since you don't have to work."

The pause after this is so long that Sloan and I exchange a look.

"Do you think she died in there?" Sloan whispers. I glare

at her but then hear Petunia scratching at the bedroom door to get out. It's weird for Mrs. Ivey to ignore her.

"Well, Maria, that's up to you, but I wanted to mention it." Maria is her daughter, the one who never visits, or so she tells me. "No, I know it's Charlie's senior year."

Another pause.

I peel a trash bag off the stack and shake it loose, trying not to listen, but it's hard. Charlie is Maria's son, Mrs. Ivey's grandson. They live somewhere over in Georgia, I think.

"You know how hard your daddy's birthday is on me. No, I'm not— I just miss you both. I thought we could—" She stops, and I can't tell if she's collecting her thoughts or Maria is talking over her.

Mrs. Ivey's a proud lady. Her house might be small, but she likes things just so. It kills me to hear her begging her own daughter for a visit. After another minute, Mrs. Ivey says, "I know, I know. I love you too. Bye now." She finally lets out Petunia, who gallops toward us like a tiny racehorse, and Sloan and I scatter to opposite ends of the kitchen so we don't look like the eavesdroppers we are.

I'm on my hands and knees by the front door Windexing Petunia's nose prints off the glass when I hear Sloan in the living room ask, "What you got there, Mrs. Ivey?"

"This, my dear, is a tennis bracelet. Harold bought it for me for our sixtieth wedding anniversary."

I sit back on my heels to get a better view. Mrs. Ivey is dangling a sparkling bracelet in the air. When Petunia makes a leap for the bracelet, Mrs. Ivey swats at her.

"That's real pretty. My mom has one like it," Sloan says.

"Your mother has good taste."

"Oh, she knows it."

Mrs. Ivey chuckles. "I'm not one for the fancy stuff, but my Harold said I deserved something extra special for our diamond wedding anniversary. I'd forgotten all about it until my daughter asked after it."

Sloan sits down on the coffee table, knocking over the magazines I stacked up not five minutes ago. "Sixty is a lot of years to be married to a person."

"It sure is." Mrs. Ivey cups the bracelet like a hurt bird.

"You want me to put it on you?" Sloan offers.

Mrs. Ivey shakes her head. I watch as she drapes the chain over her tiny wrist and begins to fumble with the clasp. I don't realize I'm holding my breath until it falls into her lap. She pounds the arm of her chair with a fist. "I can't seem to get it situated." Her voice wobbles.

"You got a paper clip?" Sloan asks.

Mrs. Ivey points to the little tray that holds her TV remote and a box of tissues. Sloan rummages around in the loose change, lifts out a clip, and unbends it so that it's in the shape of an S.

"All right, so if you hook this end of the paper clip into

the loop of your bracelet, you can hold it in place while you use your other hand to work the clasp." She demonstrates on herself before passing over the bracelet dangling from the end of the clip like a worm on a hook.

Mrs. Ivey hesitates. "Harold was always my zipper and clasper. When you've been married so long, you get used to relying on somebody else to do the little things for you."

Sloan sets the bracelet down. "My mom taught me this trick." She pauses. "My dad works a lot. I guess she had to figure out how to do it herself."

They sit there, staring at the bracelet between them, and it feels like a moment I'm not invited to witness. I study the swirls in the wood floor for something else to look at, until Mrs. Ivey snaps her fingers, making me jump.

"Give me that thing," she demands. Sloan passes over the paper-clipped bracelet.

When she finally gets it after a couple of tries, Sloan claps. Mrs. Ivey holds the bracelet up so that it catches the afternoon light and sends sparkles across the floor like a starburst.

It's strange, the things you learn when you clean someone's house. I know the Kusels are vegetarian but wish they weren't, based on all the plant-based burgers and soy sausage they consume. I know Mr. Ellsworth never eats dinner with his family, because there's always a separate container in the fridge with his name on it and instructions for heating. And now I know Mrs. Ivey has a diamond bracelet in a drawer that she couldn't put on without the husband who gave it to her.

I'm an accidental detective, because what you own and how you treat it says a lot about you. I wonder if people would keep hiring cleaners if they knew we know all their secrets.

I am turning back toward the front door and pretending to rewipe the Petunia smudges when Sloan jogs down the hallway.

"Wrap it up, Fran." She nudges me with her knee and then pulls out her phone and does not help me put away the cleaning supplies. When we leave, though, I catch her looking back at Mrs. Ivey.

"You know," I say when we get outside, "you're actually kind of nice when you want to be."

"I have no idea what you're talking about," she says, but then pockets her phone and pulls out two of the orange hard candies Mrs. Ivey keeps in a glass jar by the door. She passes me one.

My hands hurt and it's still not any faster to clean with Sloan's help, but she didn't bother me once today about Noah or my clothes, and as we walk down the street and the sweet candy melts in my mouth, I think I might actually miss her when our three weeks is up.

All the drapes are pulled, and it's so dark when I walk into the apartment after Mrs. Ivey's that I trip over a kitchen chair and drop my backpack on my own foot. I can just barely make out the shadowy figure of Mom napping on the couch. Meg must have worn her out.

I tiptoe over and put my hand on her shoulder to see if she wants dinner.

"Get off me!"

Somebody who is *not* my mother throws off the blanket and leaps off the couch. I scream and stumble back.

A man. In our living room. A stranger. I scream again and run back to the door, where I spilled my backpack. I need my phone. It's too dark. I hit the lights.

A skinny figure in skinny jeans lets out a high-pitched wail and tugs at his hair. Derek. He darts behind the couch and crouches like an animal. I put my bag back down and look around.

Things are knocked all about. I tripped over the chair because it was knocked sideways into the kitchen. Clothes spill out of the wardrobe and onto the floor. I grab a lamp that has fallen over.

Something happened here. Where is *Mom*?

I creep around the couch with the lamp in two hands like a baseball bat because this is my home and no one gets to make me feel like this here. Derek shivers and whispers to himself. He does not look up. I use the lamp to poke him in the shoulder.

"Honey, don't," Mom says from behind me, and I jump a

foot and a half in the air. She pulls me toward her bedroom, using me as her crutch until we get there and she can fetch the real thing.

"What is going on?" I do not put down my lamp.

"Shhhh." Mom puts a finger to her lips and then leaves me by her room to go back to Derek. She holds out a hand. He takes it and lets her pull him up and lead him back to the couch, where she tucks him in like she used to do for me.

"What is Derek doing here?" I do not whisper. She hobbles back over and leads me into her room and makes me sit.

"He, uh—" Mom smooths the blanket at the foot of her bed. She's not looking at me. My knees start bumping up and down all on their own. "He was having a hard time. He came here to find Mimi, but she's gone to get groceries."

I lean back so I can see into the living room again—the narrow lump of him on the couch.

"What do you mean 'hard time'?"

"Oil Express fired him."

Mom shifts in her spot. She still won't meet my eyes. That's when I get it.

"Because he was high."

She looks at me now. How could she bring him into our house like this?

"Is he high now?" I spit the words.

She shakes her head.

"You promised no lies!" I shout. I don't care if he hears. He's a druggie stinking up our living room with his sweat and panic, and *my mom* thinks she can take care of him.

Mom struggles to stand and grabs my hand for balance. She holds on even after she's up.

"I'm not lying, Franny. He was coming down when he got here. He couldn't tell me what he took, but whatever it was, it's on its way out." She tugs my hand. "I couldn't send him away like that."

"*Yes*, you could have."

"Little D, please—"

"No, you don't get to call me that. I don't want to be the Little Dipper. I don't want to be *anything* like you." I yank my hand away so I can point at her. "You are *not* his sponsor. It's not your job to take care of him. You can barely take care of yourself!"

The words slip out before I can stop them, but even if I could, I wouldn't. The truth hurts. My heart hurts. Everything *hurts*. Mom backs away like she's been slapped.

"Franny—" Her voice is a broken thread. Before she can say more, I back into the living room. I will get Derek out of here if I have to roll him off Oscar and out the door myself. Nothing will stop me. Except one thing—the cabinet door above the sink is hanging wide open, the cabinet where I keep the BILLS jar. I run over and shove everything aside, spilling cereal all over the counter and rummaging until I feel the glass tea jar in my hand.

I check. The money's gone—*my* money I worked for, for *weeks*. I gasp and then shove everything back in because Mom is crutching her way toward me. I shut the cabinets, acting like I'm just trying to straighten up.

"Honey," she says, placing a hand on my shoulder, "let's go downstairs and wait for Mimi."

Everything I've worked for. Gone.

I pause as Mom unlocks Mimi's door with her key. Derek is still here. Which means if he took the money, it's still here too. I look up the darkened stairwell. If I don't want to let some druggie waste everything I've worked for, I'm going to have to go up there and get it back.

It takes Mom ages to fall asleep. Long after Mimi has gone upstairs to "tend to Derek," Mom tosses and turns, creating a symphony of creaks on Mimi's old twin bed. Me? I'm still as a stone. You'd think I fell into a coma. Except my brain is whirring with so many variables, I'm surprised smoke isn't coming out my ears. What if Mimi is awake up there? What if *Derek* is? Am I seriously going to have to search him? And also, how do I do that?

But what choice do I have? I think of all that cash and huff into my pillow. It was more than I've ever seen in my entire life. When I held it in my hand, it felt less like paper and more like an actual weight that could anchor us to a better life. If Mom had ever bothered to look past the Rice Krispies, she would have had to wonder where it all came from, and then I'd have gotten caught. If I get that money back, I'm burying it in the backyard or under my mattress.

Finally, long after midnight, Mom starts to snore—something she swears she never does, but how would she know? I unbend my legs, which are stiff from pretending to sleep. Then I carefully climb off the couch and creep out of Mimi's apartment and up the stairs, a burglar in my own house.

At the top stair I freeze. Blue light spills from the crack in the door to our apartment. At first I think Derek's on his phone, but when I nudge the door wider, I see it's the light from the neon sign out front. Mimi has opened the blinds and the windows to let in a little air.

Derek is still passed out on the couch. I can see the tips of his bleached hair sticking out from the top of the blanket. Mimi, thankfully, is slumped over in a chair at the kitchen table, fast asleep over a cup of cold coffee. That woman could snooze anywhere.

I hold my breath and tiptoe over to the couch. Poor Oscar. He doesn't deserve this—Derek sweating all his toxins out on him. As carefully as I can in the half-light, I tug down the blanket. Underneath it, Derek is nothing but skin and bones in a ratty white undershirt and too-big jeans.

I reach out my hand toward the pocket of those jeans. Then pull back. *Breathe, Franny, breathe. In for four. Out for four.* Huh, I feel calmer. It actually works. I guess Mom's breathing techniques come in handy after all.

Steadier now, I check his back pockets. There's nothing there but a half-squished pack of Camels. Great. I'm going to have to search his front pockets. And he's lying on his stomach. Maybe I could just kind of . . . flip him like a pancake. He's light enough, and clearly totally out of it. I reach forward, but right as my fingertips touch his shoulder, Derek whimpers in his sleep and I jerk back, my heart scrabbling around in my throat.

I sit on my heels and rub my head. I can't do it. If the money's there, it's as good as gone. Derek did this. But also, Mom did this by letting him inside in the first place. This is what addiction does. It destroys everything it touches. It's not fair. This shouldn't have to be our life. And right when I was trying to make it better, it goes to pieces again.

I look around, the blue light of the sign revealing everything I couldn't see earlier. A hinge on our wardrobe is broken, and it hangs crooked like a chipped tooth. Mom's favorite box of thread has spilled. Spools of lime- and emerald- and moss-green lie in a big messy pile under the sewing machine. The rug is covered in crusty mud from Derek's boots.

Derek's *boots*. I tell myself not to get my hopes up, except that they are already up because this is my last shot. I crawl over to where they sit by the foot of the couch and reach my hand way down inside the right one. Down, down, until my fingers hit the tip. Nothing. I huff. Mimi snuffles in her sleep. But when I sneak a glance at her, she's out, her head thrown back and her mouth open wide.

Right, one boot down, one to go. Odds are fifty-fifty. I cross my fingers with one hand and use the other to dig around in the left one. Crinkly something! Definitely not a sock! I yank and hold my treasure to the light—a wad of twenties, *my* twenties! It's the most glorious thing I have ever seen. I cover my mouth so I don't yelp.

Okay, time to get out of here. I shove the money into my pocket, where it belongs, and start to turn away, but I can't leave it like this. Derek came into my home, messed with my things, messed with my mom. He shouldn't get off so easy. I grab a Post-it and a Sharpie from the clutter under the coffee table and dash off a quick note to our dear friend Derek and shove it in his shoe.

Dear Derek,
I have taken the money back.
Forget making amends.
Get out of our lives.
Franny
P.S. This stays between us.

23

THE NEW DEAL

WEDNESDAY, APRIL 2

Math: Turn in blue folder (hooray!)

Mrs. Ivey's: Sloan's last day :(

SKIP NA/AA MEETING

BY MORNING, DEREK IS GONE and our apartment is back to normal—everything in its place. Both Mom and Mimi try to talk to me about "the incident" all weekend. But no amount of deep breathing or counting Cs is going to make me forget that Mom let him bring his chaos into our lives. And even though I meant everything I said about not wanting to be like her, it still twists my stomach to think about it. I wish life weren't such a tangled mess. I wish my mom could be my mom and I could be a kid and the roles didn't keep flip-flopping. Then I wouldn't have to wake up every day wondering which version of Franny I have to be.

I sigh and shove the BILLS jar all the way to the back of the wall underneath my bed. I've started counting the money three, sometimes four times a day. That and writing in my planner are the only things that stop the worry.

Opening my planner, I put a sad face next to the note about Sloan. I know I should be dancing around the apartment singing "Hallelujah!" now that she'll finally be gone. I've caught her sitting in the Ellsworths' bathroom and typing on her phone a million times. She still hasn't learned to properly clean a mirror, and she always makes me carry out the heaviest bags of trash. And she won't do any of the extra probability homework I've made for her. I don't want to care about Sloan, but now I've gotten used to having her around.

I'm eating the last of the off-brand Fruity Pebbles with no milk because we're out when I hear Mom on Mimi's phone.

"Yes, tonight works." Pause. "Absolutely! So sorry I haven't returned it." Loooooong pause. "Six it is." Mom hops up next to me on her crutch. "You take care too, now. Bye."

She steals a handful of cereal and winks at me. This is what she does—gets all jokey when she should be acting sorry. I pull the Fruity Pebbles out of her reach.

"Who was that?"

"Ruthann Bedford."

"The *church* lady? Why'd she call?"

"I called her. We've had her casserole dish for weeks, and Mimi refuses to take it to her. She's coming tonight to pick it up."

"Mimi's going to love that."

Mom snorts. Her hair is clean and tucked under a lavender bandana. The hollows beneath her eyes have disappeared too. She looks almost like she did before the crash.

She grabs the cereal box from me, shakes it, and frowns when she finds it empty.

"We're out of food," I add unnecessarily.

"Nope." She shakes her head. "Mimi restocked us. I just didn't get around to bringing it up from her place this weekend. Meg says pretty soon I can ditch this thing." She taps the crutch that she's wrapped in a rainbow of yarn. It looks like something you'd check out of the My Little Pony hospital. "And you can stop making my lunch, you know."

Ouch. "But I've always made your lunch," I say.

"I know, honey. But it feels good to do things for myself again." She tugs on one of my curls and smiles. I don't. I should be relieved—one less thing to do—but it feels like a loss, like someone took away my extra credit before it was done.

"I'm thinking of calling up my regulars again too. I need to tell them I'll be back to light work in a few weeks. I won't be able to do full cleans, but it's better than nothing."

My heart hits the accelerator.

"When you get home," she adds, digging around in the pantry, "would you copy down all those telephone numbers for the regulars that are in your planner? I'm going to call them tonight."

She pulls out an almost-empty jar of Jif and grabs a spoon.

"Uh—sure." I push my half-full bowl toward her. I'm not so hungry anymore.

She points at the sunshine clock on the wall with her peanut-buttery spoon.

"You better hustle, baby. You're gonna be late."

Mr. Jamison is at his desk elbow-deep in a giant plastic box of what look like Legos. This is not the strangest thing he's done in the name of learning. As I get closer, I notice they're all in a big jumble. My hands itch to sort them. But I have more important business. I need something to cheer me up after this morning's conversation with Mom. And nothing cheers me up like a task completed.

"Here, sir," I say, holding out the blue folder.

He raises his eyebrows. "You finished it? Already?"

I nod and hold back a smile.

He unearths a hand from the bin and takes it. "There's hard stuff in here. I threw in some concepts they don't cover until high school." He flips through the folder, not really reading, just skimming. The rustling pages send a breeze my way. It's the best feeling in the world. "I thought it would take you the rest of the year."

I impressed Mr. Jamison. Surprised him, even. Despite Mom's injury and the cleaning and the *unexpected* houseguest, I still did the work and did it well. I give up on not smiling—I couldn't hold it back now if I tried. Things have been hard enough. I deserve this.

"Is it your birthday?" Noah asks as I take my seat at the table. "'Cause you look extra happy."

"Nope, not my birthday. Just a regular old good day."

I toss him a smile and he tosses one back. His yellow hoodie brings out the flecks of gold in his brown eyes.

"So, have you made any new animals lately?" I ask, feeling brave.

"As a matter of fact . . ." He digs in his bag and lifts out a box like the ones Mom uses to store her thread. When he opens it, I see a pile of paper all the colors of the rainbow—deep green and bright purple and crimson and teal. On top of those are several half-folded sheets—works in progress, I guess. He pulls out an orange one and cups it in his hands so I can't see it.

"Wow, you're really serious about this stuff." I point at the box.

"Oh, there's nothing serious about this, Frances," he says in a mock Mr. Jamison tone. "Truth is, I like it, so I do it."

I get that. I'd still do math even if math class didn't exist.

"Do the basketball guys make fun of you?" I ask, which is maybe not the right thing to say. I don't want him to think *I* think he should be embarrassed by it.

"Yeah," he says, and then shrugs. "But who cares, right?"

I nod like I understand, but I don't. How does he let other people's opinions roll off him like that? I wish I could. But every jab sticks to me like lint in the dryer.

"Here." Noah holds out his hand with the orange paper, so I hold out mine to take it.

It's a fox, staring at me with pointy ears that make him look alert, like he's excited about something. His tail even has a white tip. I can already picture him next to the turtle and the bird on my windowsill.

"Cool," I say. I hand it back, but I don't want to.

"No, no! It's for you!" He returns it, his hands cupped around mine for just a second.

"Thank-you-he's-beautiful," I say in one long breath.

Noah's face breaks into a happy grin. I guess he cares a little bit about what other people say.

"Thought it'd be appropriate." He taps his forehead. "Foxes are sly."

I remember what Mom asked me about her clients' numbers this morning. "Sly" can mean "smart," but it can also mean "sneaky." I feel more sneaky than smart these days. Still, I set the fox carefully on top of my planner as Sloan slides in between us.

"Cutting it kind of close," I joke, because in the weirdest turn of life events, I can now tease Sloan. She pretends to fan herself with her homework.

"I was finishing this. Did the work by myself . . . without

'help,' I might add." The air quotes around "help" say every-thing. She wants me to know she didn't cheat. I give her a shoulder bump. This is where we are now—I can hassle her for almost being late and not worry about having my back-pack kicked across the room. It's a not-so-minor miracle.

Sloan spots the fox and grabs it.

"Careful there," Noah says from her other side.

"Did *you* make this?" she asks him.

"I did," he answers in a tone that says *I dare you to make fun of it.*

To her credit, she says, "Nice tail," and passes it back to me, her mouth already forming a million questions. I give her my best *we will talk about this later* glare and do not dare look at Noah for the rest of class.

24

IT'S COMPLICATED

THE AFTERNOON AT MRS. IVEY'S goes too fast. Sloan takes Petunia for a walk while I sweep the pine needles from the patio. It's awkward moving the broom around Mrs. Ivey while she watches me from under her straw hat. It's four p.m. and she's already in her pink housecoat, with the snaps done up wrong.

"So, Franny, tell me," she says, and then pauses so long I think she's fallen asleep, before finishing with "How *is* the remodel going?"

"The what?" I stop and lean against the broom.

"The re-mo-del at the laun-dro-mat," she yells, enunciating each syllable like it's me who's hard of hearing.

Oops. I forgot that was the excuse I gave for Mom not being around. With so many lies, it's hard to remember which ones I planted where.

"Oh, right! It's good! Almost done, I think." I pick up the broom and pretend to sweep a spot next to the back door so I don't have to meet her eye. I can feel her watching me.

"Well, that's nice to hear," she says after the longest minute of my life. She rocks in her patio chair, and my heart beats a nervous rhythm with every squeak of the springs. "It'll be nice to catch up with your mama . . . when she's back."

"Uh-huh." I need an escape. "Can I get you something to drink? One of those Lipton teas?"

"That'd be lovely, dear."

I flee to the kitchen and stand in front of the refrigerator for a few minutes to collect myself. Mom said she's ready to get back to work in a few weeks. Mrs. Ivey is surely going to ask her about the "remodel." What level of terrible would I be to tell Mom it was a misunderstanding and blame it on Mrs. Ivey's old age?

Sloan gets back from her walk with Petunia as I'm coming inside again with Mrs. Ivey's empty glass.

"It is hooooot out there. Way too hot for March. Gym camp this summer is going to be a beast if it keeps going up from here," Sloan says, getting down an extra bowl to fill with water for Petunia, who is panting with exhaustion or excitement. Mrs. Ivey never walks her more than the three feet it takes her to "do her business" before hightailing it back into the house.

Sloan's sleeveless shirt says SWOOSH, and her hair is up in a messy bun that I could never pull off. My hair's so poufy, it'd make me look like I was growing an extra head.

"So . . . ," she says, eyeing me over her glass of water.

"Sew buttons."

"What?"

"It's something my mom says whenever anybody starts off a sentence like that."

Sloan snorts into her water glass. Three weeks ago I never would have said something that goofy to anybody, especially not Sloan. I can't believe today is her last day. A jolt of sadness shoots through me.

"*So*, I need an update." At my blank look, she adds, "On *Noah*. Come on. I can't do *all* the work for you."

"Uh—"

"Oh, enough said."

"What?"

"Nothing. Your face says it all. You haven't even tried to flirt with him after our Sonic rehearsal, have you?"

"He's not . . . I don't—"

Sloan pokes me in the shoulder. Mean Sloan and nice Sloan both like to poke. "Come on. What's the holdup? We both know you like him."

"I don't have time to like him!" I say, rinsing out the glasses and loading them into the dishwasher. There are only two plates and one butter knife in there, but I set the cycle to clean. There's nothing sadder than a dishwasher that never gets filled.

She folds her arms.

"Noah likes you. You like him. You both could skip

work, hang out after school, have a little *fun*. It doesn't have to be complicated."

It *is* complicated. No work means no paycheck. No paycheck means no money in the jar. And no money in the jar means Mom and me crawling back to Memphis, where all the bad memories live. But I can't say any of that. Even if Sloan and I are maybe-friends, she doesn't know my secrets. She doesn't understand how poor we are and what happens on Wednesday nights when the laundromat closes early. She only knows a slice of me, and it's a carefully measured one.

Sloan shakes her head when I stay mute. "At least swap seats with me in math. If you can't flirt, you can get an inch closer."

I don't say yes. But I don't say no, either. Sloan smirks while we gather the cleaning supplies and actually helps me put them away. She doesn't have to ask where anything goes. We could do this in our sleep now.

As we step outside, my chest tightens. In about thirty seconds, Sloan will turn left to catch the uptown bus toward her Royal Oaks neighborhood and I will turn right to walk the three blocks to the laundromat. And then that's it.

"Well," I say, and hold out my hand, because I don't know what else to do, even though nobody shakes hands anymore. I wonder if it's too late to turn it into a fist bump. She looks down at my hand, then up at me. Definitely too late.

"Blackmail over, then?" she asks.

"According to our agreement, you've fulfilled your side of the bargain, so yes." I nod. "Blackmail officially over." I sound like an alien version of myself. *Hel–lo, my name is Fran–ces. I come in peace.* I stare down at my hand, still held out. The knuckles aren't cracked as bad now that Sloan's been helping. My heart sinks.

"So," she begins, "I was thinking . . ."

I risk a quick glance up at her. She's staring at the sidewalk.

"Yeah?" A tiny bubble of hope begins to rise before I can squash it. Maybe we can still be friends even after the "arrangement" is over? Friends for real.

"*So,* I still need help if I'm going to pass math and get into gym camp. And you are obviously still in need of my super-smooth moves if we're going to get you and Noah to talk about anything other than construction-paper animals."

"He doesn't use construction paper."

"Not the point. The point is, you need my help too."

"I do?"

There's that hope again, flapping around in my chest like a bird.

"Well, *obviously.* So I'm proposing a new deal: I'll keep cleaning with you if you keep tutoring me. Deal?"

She holds out her hand. I stare at it. *So* much of me wants to take it. But I shake my head.

"I can't."

Sloan's shoulders slump, and her hand falls just like mine did.

"*Fine.* I didn't think teaching me how to graph was such *torture.*"

"It's not! That's not what I meant!"

I want her to look at me, because if she did, maybe she'd see what I was trying to say without me having to find the words. But she's back to studying the sidewalk. I know, like you know the split second before the popcorn burns, that if I don't speak *now*, Sloan will walk away and that will be the end.

"I will still help you with math!" I blurt out. "I love that stuff. You know that!"

"You will?" Sloan looks confused. It's understandable. I just said two opposite things: no, I can't make this deal, and yes, I'll help you with math. For someone who always likes things to make sense, I'm not doing such a hot job of it.

"I mean I'll do it, but I'll do it for free," I explain. "You don't have to help me clean. It feels wrong to take payment for something I like to do anyway. Tutoring is . . . kind of fun." *And also, I want us to be friends without having to bargain for it,* I think. But you can't say that kind of stuff to a maybe-friend. That's a BFF, secret-spilling, note-passing, clothes-trading kind of confession, and Sloan and I are *so* not on that level.

She looks me up and down like she's trying to tell if I'm messing with her. I guess I deserve that.

"First of all," she says, "that's weird. Who likes to teach other people *math*? Second of all, what if I come along to help clean anyway? Mrs. Ivey is cool, in a retro, *Golden Girls* kind of way. Also, it turns out cleaning is great conditioning for gymnastics."

She flexes her biceps, and I laugh, mostly with relief.

"Okay, yeah. Okay. I mean, only if you want to. But yeah, that'd be great." *Stop talking, Franny!*

"Cool. We're good." She holds out her hand and I move to shake it, but she slaps it in a high five instead and laughs. "You gotta stop taking everything so *seriously*, Frances," she says. Then she punches me in the arm for good measure.

25.

DRAMA

WHEN I WALK INTO the apartment, Ruthann is squared off against Mimi in our kitchen again. Her hair is even brighter than before, if that's possible. It looks like a red bike helmet. Which might come in handy. Mimi has a wrench in her hand. This should be good.

"You have no right!" Mimi shouts at a volume that seems unnecessary.

Ruthann doesn't blink.

Mom sits at our tiny kitchen table, which we have never eaten at once. It's actually lawn furniture and mostly holds mail and magazines and whatever else gets dropped there on the way from the door to the couch. She looks delighted.

"All we need is popcorn," she says, patting the chair next to her. I sit and settle in for the show.

"It is *absolutely* my right!" Mimi yells. "Jules is like my own flesh and blood, and this is asking too much."

I glance back at Mom. She winks at me.

Ruthann is holding the casserole dish with the "Return Me" Post-it I stuck on it weeks ago.

"This is between me and Julia," she says now.

"Ruthann has been kind enough to offer me some work," Mom says, filling me in on the drama.

"What kind of work?" I ask. Despite Mimi's face right now, which looks like she's sucking on a Sour Patch Kid, this might be a good thing. Maybe it'll pay decent money and we can finally quit cleaning and scraping around for odd jobs.

"The kind of work that is too taxing for someone in your mother's condition," Mimi says, waving the wrench in the air.

"I'd hardly call making a few costumes for the Easter play taxing," Mom replies calmly.

Oh, great. Because there's *so much money* in costumes. This is exactly why I started the secret jar. Mom doesn't think logically about things. She just takes whatever work drifts by. That's the difference between a job and a *career*. A career is something you can talk about in front of your kid's schoolmates without people laughing.

Plus, Easter is my least favorite holiday of the year. Mom of all people should understand that. I sit on my hands to keep still and close my eyes against the memory that's bubbling up. It's no use. I'm sucked back three years ago, to another spring and the absolute *worst* Before.

• • • •

We'd been living with my grandparents for almost four years by the time the worst spring of our lives rolled around.

Grandma Jean and Grandpa were nice enough, but they never really warmed to me. Mom was supposed to go to school, graduate in four years, and get a real job, not get pregnant her freshman year and then limp her way through community college for almost a decade. I wasn't part of the plan. So they signed me up for all the low-cost after-school activities they could think of to get me out of the house— basketball at the rec center, even though I hate sports, and cleaning at the animal shelter, even though I'm allergic to cats. They wanted me busy and gone.

Somehow, even with all the drugs and the stopping and starting, Mom had made it to her last semester of school. She was almost done. We were going to have a big celebration in May when she *finally* received her diploma. What none of us talked about, because my grandparents are not people who talk about things, was that Mom was obviously still doped up half the time.

She'd come home late and fumble with her key in the lock. Her speech would be slurred when she woke me up to say good night. She rarely looked right at me, but when she did, whatever she saw made her cry. Everything made her cry back then. I'd hear her on the other side of the bathroom door, even though she would turn the water on to drown it out.

Easter weekend was one of the few times we all went to church, and that year Grandma splurged on a dress for me at Dillard's. It was yellow with rabbits stitched along the bottom. I didn't like it. It looked like a baby's dress. But Mom smiled when she saw it, so I pretended to love it too.

The Wednesday before Easter was cloudy and hotter than normal. The air felt that kind of heavy that settles on your shoulders. I had just gotten home from school and was putting my bag down when the phone rang. Grandpa answered it from the den. I couldn't hear anything he said, but he wasn't on the phone two minutes before he hung up and yelled for Grandma Jean.

They left in a rush, telling me to lock the door and that there was egg salad in the fridge. They didn't say what had happened, but I knew it was Mom. It had to be. She was the only emergency in our family.

I skipped dinner and sat in the empty bathtub, cradling the house phone and waiting for them to call. The next morning, Grandma Jean found me in the tub and woke me up. It was barely light. They had just gotten home.

"Frances," she said, because she never called me Franny. "Your mother took too many of those pills yesterday. She's okay now and having a rest at the hospital." She was sitting on the toilet and paused to tear off a piece of toilet paper. I waited for her to cry or blow her nose, but she just balled it up in her hand. If she wasn't crying, I felt like I couldn't either. "We'll visit her this weekend," she said, then patted my shoulder, stood up, and left.

By Easter, Mom had been moved to a rehab center, one she'd never been to before. It was newer and had a pond out front with geese running zigzags on the lawn. I was afraid of the geese. One darted at me, honking and snapping its beak at the hem of my yellow dress.

We found Mom sitting in a white wooden chair under the shade of a cherry tree. She looked so skinny. There were circles under her eyes and new hollows in her cheeks.

"Oh, baby, you look lovely!" she said, and then she started to sob. It was such a loud sound in this quiet place that it scared me and I started crying too. My grandparents mumbled something about taking a walk around the grounds and beat a quick retreat toward the pond and the crazy geese.

Mom stopped crying before I did and opened her arms to me. I was too old for it, but I crawled into her lap and she kissed the top of my head.

We didn't say anything for the longest time. We listened to the sounds of geese honking until someone with a clipboard led a group of little kids down the path in front of us. They were clutching Easter baskets, and their parents trailed behind, all wearing plastic hospital wristbands like Mom. The leader blew a whistle and the kids started screaming and running all over the place, hunting for plastic eggs.

"You want to join them?" Mom asked.

I shook my head. I couldn't think of anything I'd rather do less. These kids were acting like it was recess when it felt more like a funeral.

While the cherry tree dropped its pink blossoms on us, I leaned back into Mom and tried to catch her old scent—cinnamon Jolly Ranchers and mint toothpaste. It was still there under the hospital smell.

"I made you something," she said, and pulled a plastic grocery bag out from under her chair.

Inside was a Post-it with a sketch of the Big Dipper and Little Dipper inside a heart. It was stuck to a tiny square of fabric stitched with the words "You + Me = Love" in purple. It was a little wrinkled from being in the bag, but I hugged it to me and slipped the Post-it into the pocket of my dress.

Right then my grandparents came walking back from the pond and said we had to go. Grandma Jean didn't want the ham she'd cooked to go to waste.

Before she let me go, Mom leaned down and whispered, "Never again, Franny. I'm clean, and I will never leave you again."

I didn't believe her. Why should I, with the number of times I'd heard that before? But after a month at the rehab center with the pond, she checked herself out and quit school, and we left Memphis for good. She's been drug-free ever since. I still hate Easter.

• • • •

"Oh, it's not just any play," Ruthann is explaining to me now. "The Pageant Wagon goes all out this time of year. That's the little church theater troupe I've put together."

Mimi snorts.

"I am *also* part of the community theater in town, which is not affiliated with the church," Ruthann continues. "They have agreed to give us some of their costumes. But it's mostly Elizabethan. You know, Lady Macbeth and lacy collars and corsets." She fake shivers. "Hardly appropriate for the resurrection of Christ. That's where your mother comes in."

Mom is sitting up straight with both legs bent at the knee. You wouldn't even know she was hurt if it weren't for the rainbow crutch by her side. She's watching me closely. I can tell she's already decided to do it, but she still wants me to say yes.

I turn to Ruthann. "What's it pay?"

"Franny!" Mom shouts.

"Thatta girl," Mimi cheers.

Ruthann studies her casserole dish. "Well, since we don't charge for attendance, this would, ah, be a strictly volunteer position."

"So no money, then."

"Franny, that's enough," Mom says, her voice a warning. I hold up my hands, like *no harm done*, before I get myself grounded for the first time in my life. But seriously, how can she think this is a good idea? I've checked the insurance statements and hospital bills she leaves lying on the kitchen table. They aren't going away. This all seems like a waste of time to me. On the upside, if it keeps her busy enough not to call up her cleaning clients tonight and buys me some more time, then fine. I paste on a smile.

"Sounds fun." Because it *sure* doesn't sound like work.

Ruthann claps her hands, and Mimi lets the wrench fall into the sink with a thunk.

"Fantastic! I'll stop by tomorrow with the costumes we already have, and maybe we can sort through some of the fabrics to see if we can't make them a little less *medieval*," Ruthann says. Mom grabs her crutch and heaves herself up to show her to the door. She wobbles for a second, and I fight the urge to hold on to her elbow. If she wanted my help, she would have asked.

"Well, that's just great," Mimi says once Ruthann is gone. "I *know* this is Carl's idea."

"You have to tell us now. What's your deal with Pastor Carl?" Mom teases. She sits back down at the table and begins folding a piece of quilting fabric.

"There is no *deal*," Mimi says. "Let's just say I knew *Pastor* Carl before he knew the Lord, and he had a *very* different idea of a good time."

"Ohhhhh," Mom says, leaning back in her chair. "Mimi and Carl, sittin' in a tree, *K-I-S-S-I-N-G*."

"That's enough of that," Mimi says, and starts banging around under the sink with the wrench to drown Mom out.

I make up some excuse about homework to escape to my room. All the good feelings from earlier have dissolved. I turned in the blue folder. Noah gave me a fox. Sloan still wants to hang out. But all I can think now is . . . *my mother is never going to grow up.* When she goes downstairs for her Wednesday-night meeting, I check the kitchen drawer. The bottle of pills is still there, but that doesn't settle my mind.

I wasn't going to eavesdrop. I really wasn't. But I can't help it. If I want any kind of real honesty from Mom, I'm going to have to get it the sneaky way. I press my ear to the door and listen.

"—that he can just come in here after acting like that. It ain't right. We—"

"Pete," Mimi interrupts.

"No. We've all lost jobs, spouses, gotten knocked around, but we don't bring our business to each other's doorsteps."

I peek through the round window. Pete pounds his knee with his fist. He's normally soft-spoken. I've never seen him so worked up.

"Look at Julia. She got busted up real bad, but she's not using it as an excuse to use. You"—he points at Derek, who is hunched over in his seat with his head hanging down—"got no *excuse.*"

Derek. I *told* him to stay away. They must all know by now what happened on Friday. About him showing up here high and Mom having to take care of him. *Go get 'im, Pete.*

"Pete," Mom says so softly, I can barely hear. She holds a white bandana in her hands. "He came here looking for Mimi. He was trying to get help."

"You ask for help *before* you stick that needle in your arm, son. Not after," Pete says. "You think it wasn't hard on me? My wife left me. My kids won't speak to me. I got a grandbaby I've never seen. All because I couldn't lift my head out of the bottle long enough to be the man I should have been when they needed me. I've been sober eight years, and they've been *lonely* years. And still, I don't pick Jack for company." He sighs like he's disgusted with this whole business. "Even if I did, I wouldn't go cry on the shoulder of another addict who's struggling."

Derek's head dips lower, if that's even possible, like he's a dog that's been kicked. I steel myself against the tiny bit of pity I feel for him. He trashed our apartment! He stole from me! He shouldn't get sympathy.

"He did the right thing," Mrs. Lois says now. She looks like she's feeling pretty bad for Derek too. Her knitting needles are drooping in her lap. "He made a mistake and he came to Mimi for help."

"Don't change the fact that he dragged Julia into it," Pete argues.

"We don't judge here," Mimi says.

Mom lifts herself from her seat and hops to the one next to Derek. His shoulders are shaking.

"We've all made mistakes we thought were unforgivable," she says.

Pete's voice is softer when he turns to Mom, but the words aren't. "Yeah, but we've got to call it what it is. If he don't want to even try, then he don't need to be here."

"Pete—" Mom and Mrs. Lois say at the same time.

Derek jumps up, his chair skidding back half a foot.

"He's right. I *shouldn't* be here!" He glances around the circle, and I swear he catches my eye. "What's the point? I quit."

I watch him flee from my porthole window.

26

FALSE EQUATIONS

MONDAY, APRIL 14

Switch seats with Sloan (her idea)

Ask for more extra credit from Mr. J?

Avoid Mom and all talk of Easter play AT ALL
  COSTS

THE POSTER IS IMPOSSIBLE to miss. It's a giant pastel explosion of flowers and glitter plastered over everything else on the library bulletin board.

"Spring Bash. Who names a dance the Spring *Bash*?" I wonder out loud.

"Ms. Taylor, that's who," Sloan answers. We're standing in the middle of a crowd of girls already talking higher and faster at the prospect of dress buying.

"Well, it sounds violent," I say, and turn away.

Sloan snorts, then elbows me right between the ribs. "You should ask Noah."

"Umm, *no*. A few origami animals does not mean he likes me."

"Umm, *yes*, it does. And you would be cute together. If you're worried about the dancing part, he's tall enough you could stand on his feet. He could waltz you around like his tiny bleach-smelling puppet."

"Ha ha. Wait—" I stop in the middle of the hall on our way to math. "Do I really smell like bleach?" I sniff my shirt, but all I catch is the scent of strawberry from the Pop-Tart I had for breakfast.

"There are worse things to smell like, Franny," Sloan says. "Don't chicken out of the Plan. We're trading seats today so you can sit next to him."

I swallow. The Plan. Which is in the planner. Which means I have to do it. Except now it seems impossible. It's an explosion of awkward waiting to happen. Our elbows will keep bumping. We'll lean over at the same time to get something out of our bags and knock heads. He'll start to say something and I'll start to say something and then both of us will know *what* to say—like that sidestepping thing you do in the hall when you're trying to go around somebody and then they step the same way, so neither of you can pass.

"About that—" I begin, but Sloan runs ahead of me like we're in a race. She's going to set up this seating arrangement with or without me. I would hide in the library and skip class altogether, except I really, *really* want to ask Mr. Jamison for more extra credit.

When I get to math, Sloan is predictably already in my old seat. She winks so hugely, Noah would have to be in a coma to miss it. But he's not looking at her. He's looking at me, and he's smiling, like he's happy with this new development. I order all the muscles in my face not to grin back, but then I do.

Maybe this isn't such a bad idea. Maybe this will keep me from thinking about Derek and about Mom's new "job" on my least favorite holiday. She was up before the sun, the sewing machine whirring louder than the washing machines downstairs.

I turn away from the drama at my table and aim for Mr. Jamison instead. He's organizing a bunch of pick-up sticks by color on his desk. I bet he has a closet at home like Mom's sewing closet, except it's filled with math games. I would love to have a closet like that. He doesn't notice me until I clear my throat.

"Oh, Franny, good," he says distractedly. "Will you look under there and see if you can spot an orange one? A few have gotten away from me."

I get down on my hands and knees and find an orange stick, plus a blue one and a green one, too, under his desk.

He is delighted. "Thank you!"

"You're welcome, sir."

He goes back to sorting, but I clear my throat again.

"Did you have a question?" he asks without looking up.

"Yes, sir. I just wondered if you had any more extra credit for me since I finished the blue folder so fast." I hope it doesn't sound like I'm bragging.

He straightens up and resettles his glasses on his nose but doesn't speak. Why isn't he saying anything?

Slowly, like we've hit half speed on a video, he bends down and opens his desk drawer. Then he pulls out the blue folder and hands it to me. I take it by reflex. Why is he giving me the same work I've already done?

"About that," he begins, and an alarm goes off in my brain. "You did some excellent work all the way through integers and proportional relationships." He pauses. The alarm gets louder. "But if you'll remember, I stuck some really difficult stuff in there—higher-level word problems and graphing for function. That's advanced, even for ninth grade."

My thoughts bang around like moths at a window while I try to understand what he's saying. Proportional relationships ended halfway through the folder. Does that mean I got everything after that wrong?

"So . . . I failed?"

"Franny, no. This was *supposed* to be a challenge." He runs a hand over his head, looking deeply uncomfortable. "You are already working with concepts way past your grade level. I'm *proud* of you. Not everything has to have a grade attached to it to have value. You did good work here. Look over my notes and try again. This is a chance to learn. That's the point. Math is infinite, and that's its beauty. You can never learn everything there is to know."

He's smiling at me. Like he's excited about how many glorious wrong answers I have left to explore.

But all I hear is *I failed*. The thought bends my shoulders. I want infinite *answers*. Not infinite *problems*. I've already got enough of those.

I retreat to my table without another word. Math has always made sense when nothing else does. It's my safe place, and everybody knows I'm good at it. Now I've lost the one thing that made me, *me*. I stand in front of our table, and Sloan is in my seat and I can't remember why.

"Move," I say.

She nudges me toward her old spot instead. And winks.

Right, the Plan . . . to sit next to Noah.

I shake my head at her, but she keeps pushing me. She is *so* pushy. I pick up her bag and throw it over to her old seat.

"No," I whisper, except it's more of a shout. I can feel Noah watching us.

"Fine," Sloan says, and raises her hands, and I think it's over. For once, she's actually listening to me. Until she grabs the stupid blue folder and drops it on the ground. It lands with a splat. Noah leans over, ready to retrieve it, but Sloan steps between him and the folder and turns to face me.

"She's got it. Don't you, Franny?" she says, and then mouths *bend-and-snap*. She wiggles her eyebrows and my face burns. I snatch up the folder and hunch down in my seat—my *usual* seat, the seat reserved for failures.

"Chicken," she whispers, and that's the last thing I hear, because I spend the next forty-eight minutes of class actively not listening.

At 10:43, two minutes before the bell rings, I put my bag, which I didn't even unpack, in my lap. At the sound of the bell I race for the door, but Noah gets to me first.

"Hey, Franny."

His shirt is spring green. A happy color. It makes me want to cry.

"Hey."

Sloan hip-bumps me as she brushes past us. I know I'd catch her winking if I looked, but I don't. I can't even meet Noah's eyes. I stare at his shirt instead. His voice is a cloud that hovers over my head.

"I got some new paper from the art store and made you something."

It's probably an owl and he's going to say I'm wise. Or an elephant, because he thinks I never forget things. It should be a jellyfish—they don't even have brain cells.

But he holds up a flower. I reach out and take it, because my hand has a mind of its own. It's a yellow rose with a green stem that matches his shirt. He even added tiny twisted thorns.

"Careful," he says as I touch one. "They really are sharp."
He laughs and rubs his palms on his jeans.

"Thank you," I say through numb lips.

"You're welcome. Turn it over." His voice cracks on "over."

I do. The rose has eight petals, and on the underside of each one, he's written a word. I twirl it around slowly and read it out loud even as my stomach sinks.

"Will. You. Go. To. The. Dance. With. Me."

I spin it around again to buy some time. He doesn't know what he's asking. He doesn't know me at all. I'm not special. I can't do gymnastics like Sloan or play basketball or turn paper into art like Noah. I am the thing I never wanted to be—ordinary.

When I finally look up, his smile is like the sun. He is so happy and excited and, just, *Noah*.

"I can't."

"You can't? Or you *won't?*" he says in a voice I don't recognize.

"I can't. I have to work."

"You have to . . . work?"

It's not even a good lie. And we both know it.

"Right," he says, and grabs his bag and walks away, leaving me holding a paper flower as phony as I am.

27

WHERE IS YOUR MOTHER?

"HEY, DO YOU THINK Mrs. Ellsworth ever cooks any of the stuff in here?" Sloan holds up a box of lentil pasta and a jar of sun-dried tomatoes swimming in oil.

"I think we should stay out of her pantry." I pass Sloan the special spray for the stove, even though it's obvious the stove hasn't been used since we were last here.

"I think *you* need to stop being weird," she says, and throws a rag at me. She thinks I'm joking around, messing with her like she does with me, because she doesn't know about the blue folder or Noah asking me to the dance or the Derek incident. She doesn't know my world fell apart, *again*.

"Hey—" She climbs up on the counter to dust inside the oven vent. "Did I tell you I got a B-plus on the quiz we got back?" She holds the dusting wand up like a trophy. "I am officially a math *genius*," she declares.

"A B-plus is hardly genius." The words are out before I can stop them. Her smile slips, just like Noah's, and she looks at me like she doesn't know me. Which is the truth.

"Well, we can't all be *gifted* like you, Frances," Sloan snaps. "I'm going to clean the bathroom. That's how much I want to *not* be around you right now."

She marches down the hall, her steps ringing loudly on the wood floor. I lean against the counter and close my eyes. This is better. If I'm going to cut ties, I should do it all at once in one big chop.

Ten minutes later, when I'm done with the kitchen, I decide to find her and tell her she can go home. This new arrangement of ours isn't going to work.

"Sloan—" I begin. She's standing in the middle of the master bathroom, holding a small orange bottle up to the light. A boatload of others line the counter. The cabinet door hangs open wide.

"What are you doing?" I croak.

She doesn't flinch or try to hide the pills. She just *laughs*.

"What? You've never looked? Come on." She waves her hands over all the bottles. "Who needs this many meds?"

"Put them back." My voice is low, even though I want to scream, shove the pills back into the cabinet, and run out the door.

She narrows her eyes at me.

"No."

"*Yes.*"

"*No.*"

She starts to twist the top of one.

"Put. Them. Back!" I yell, and grab for the bottle. The lid pops off and pills go flying.

"*What* is going on here?"

Mrs. Ellsworth stands in the doorway dressed in a white tennis skirt and white sleeveless shirt. I drop to my hands and knees to scoop the tiny blue pills back into a bottle. My heart's tripping so fast, I can't breathe.

Sloan gives her a little wave. "Oh, hi, Mrs. Ellsworth."

"Sloan Tate? Why are you here?" Confusion chases anger off her face, but only for a second. She looks back at me and snaps her fingers.

"Give me those."

I get up slowly and hand her the bottle.

"We were cleaning." I point to the Windex on the counter, but that only makes Mrs. Ellsworth notice all the other bottles. She sucks in a breath and then does a full rotation of the room, taking in the mop in the corner and the bucket of rags on the floor and the shower dusted with Comet, waiting to be scrubbed.

"Franny," she says after a very long pause in which I can hear my heartbeat in my ears. "Where is your mother?"

28

COMING CLEAN

THE RIDE HOME IN THE BACK of Mimi's truck is torture. Mimi drives slower than necessary, and Mom does not turn around from her position in the passenger seat to look at me. They have chosen to pretend I don't exist. I wish I didn't.

I couldn't say goodbye to Sloan or explain anything, because Mrs. Ellsworth made her walk home immediately after she called her mother. She probably hates me. I shouldn't care. I *don't* care. I wanted a clean cut. I sure got it.

Mimi might believe in a lot of sayings, but "the customer's always right" isn't one of them. When we get to the laundromat, she kicks all the customers out, even the ones with soapy clothes in the washer and half-wet ones in the dryer. After she refunds their money so they'll stop grumbling and get out, she locks the door and flips the sign to CLOSED.

"Pull up a chair," she orders, and grabs ones for her and Mom. I place my orange chair across from them. It's like a mini version of the AA meetings I've secretly watched, except now I'm front and center, about to spill all my secrets. What a mess. I want to hide behind the door.

"This seems like as good a place as any for an intervention," Mimi says, breaking the silence. I look at Mom, who still hasn't spoken. Her bandana is a delicate square of lace that does not at all match the hard set of her jaw. Why won't she even look at me? That's not fair. After everything I've done for her, she's treating me like a criminal.

"Mom?"

"What, Franny?"

"Why aren't you saying anything?"

"I'm thinking."

We sit for another minute, Mimi and I both watching her. She's not smiling, but she's not frowning, either, which is the scariest part. She looks more serious than I've seen her in years. The clock on the wall ticks louder than ever. Finally she leans forward, her hands on her crutch like a staff.

"All right, I'm going to ask you some questions and you're going to answer them, okay?"

I nod, because what other choice do I have?

"Were you stealing medication from the Ellsworths?"

"No!"

"Don't lie to me, Frances."

"Mom, *no*. Sloan was the one who was looking at the bottles. I was trying to get her to put them back!"

"Is this the Sloan from math class? The one who bullies you? Why was she with you?"

"She's been helping me clean."

"Wait," Mimi says, holding up a hand, "what do you mean, clean? Why were you cleaning some stranger's house?"

"Not a stranger," Mom says, still looking only at me. "A client."

"So when you told us you were staying late after school, you've really been . . . *cleaning*?" Mimi leans back. I can practically hear her thought bubble: *Does not compute!*

"Yes." Lying is bad, but cleaning is good, right? Which one weighs more?

"How long?" Mom asks.

There's no point in hiding it. I slump forward.

"Since March tenth."

"March tenth!" Mom cries. "You've been cleaning the Ellsworths' house for weeks?!"

"And the Kusels' and Mrs. Ivey's," I add quietly.

"All of them?" she says, her voice high and incredulous. "You told me you called everyone and explained about my injury. You said you wanted to, and I quote, 'save me the trouble.' Did they agree to let a *child* clean their houses?" When I say nothing, her voice goes up another octave. "Do you mean to say they think *I* have been cleaning their houses all along? Have they been paying you?"

I swallow the lump in my throat and nod.

"And what did you plan to do with that money?" Mom asks, folding her arms across her chest. At the gesture, something in me snaps. It's so judgy! She has no idea how hard I've worked to keep our lives from falling apart.

"The same thing I planned to do with all the rest of the money I've been saving for the last three years—bail you out the next time something happens, because something *always* happens!"

"You've been at this for three years?"

I cross my arms. I just outed my BILLS jar. "Not the cleaning part, obviously. But yeah, birthday money, Christmas money, money the grandparents randomly send me when they feel guilty—it all goes in the jar."

Mom doesn't move. She doesn't even blink.

"I had over a thousand dollars. There'd be more, but I had to take some out for bus fare and groceries and a bathmat for Mrs. Ivey."

Mimi lets out a low whistle.

"Mimi," Mom says, turning slowly to her, "would you excuse us, please?"

"Sure thing, Jules." Mimi gets up and returns her chair to the wall as she heads back to her own apartment. Before shutting the door, she gives me a reassuring wink, but it doesn't work. Now it's just Mom and me squared off in the center of the room.

"Franny, why?" Mom asks once we are alone. Her voice

is even. I can't tell if she's mad or disappointed or tired or maybe all three.

"Because," I say, and wish I had my planner to show her the budget sheet I drew up when she first got hurt. "How are we going to pay Meg for PT and give Mimi *any* rent or ever get a new car? I've read the hospital and insurance bills. They're not getting any smaller."

"You've been checking the insurance statements?"

"Mom, we have a trickle of money coming in and a *river* of money going out. How do you think that's going to work?"

"Franny, it's not your job to—"

"Do not tell me not to worry! You don't want me to think about money or our future, but who will if I don't?"

"Me! Franny, *I* will think about all these things, and *I* will work it out. I *am* working it out. I called the hospital and set up a payment plan. And the van? Yes, it's totaled, but we had insurance on that too, and I've been watching Craigslist and CarMax for a replacement. I just haven't found the right one—the one that will *fit into our budget*, which you are so worried about."

She's been looking at cars? We *don't* have to pay back the money to the hospital all at once?

"But—"

She huffs through her nose. "No 'buts,' Franny. I *got* this." She points to me. "Little D." She points to herself. "Big D, remember?"

Us on the fire escape tracing constellations with our fingers, a concert of chirping crickets below us. The heat of summer seeping up through the warm metal slats. The feeling of safety. Of course I remember. But that was life Before and we can't ever go back there because this is After, and it's so fragile and just like Derek, anything could happen. We're always one slip away from relapse. I burst into tears.

"Oh, honey." Mom closes the distance between us faster than I've seen her move in six weeks. She wraps me in her arms, and I cry until her sleeve is soaked and my throat hurts.

"I don't want you to start doing drugs again!" I whimper into her shoulder.

"Franny, that's never going to happen. I promise."

She sits me up and smooths the hair away from my face.

"How can you promise that?"

"Because I know."

"But *how* can you know?"

"Because I wake up every day and I make that choice. I have a support system. I am *so thankful* that I have you and this place. I'm living my best life here."

I look around the laundromat, the dust bunnies in the corner and the PJ Masks sticker on dryer number seven.

"But you were supposed to get your degree and get a normal job."

Mom shakes her head. "Oh, honey, no. I tried, for your

grandparents' sake. But not everybody's meant for college and nine to five. I like the freedom of our life."

She meets my eyes. "This may sound silly to you, but I love that I can set my own schedule with the cleaning and Uber. That way I have time to be creative too." She tugs on my shirt—the white one with the giant sun she sewed onto the back. "Don't tell Mimi this, but"—she leans in and whispers—"Ruthann was on to something with these costumes. I am having a blast turning sixteenth-century undergarments into something biblical." She chuckles, and I can feel the vibrations in my shoulder where it rests against her. "I was good at school, but I never loved it. Not like you do."

That's when I remember the blue folder and my heart sinks.

"Turns out I'm not so good at school either," I say, and then I explain about the extra credit and how I can't do it and that it turns out I suck at math. "It feels like I'm failing everything at once—school, friends, the work I thought I was doing to help us out." I wipe away the tears that have started up again.

"You are not failing *anything*, Frances Bishop. Here's one thing I've learned in recovery: every day is practice for the next. You can't be perfect all the time."

She cups her hand under my chin. "I promise to stop telling you not to worry if you promise to let yourself make mistakes. It's the only way to learn. Plus, you deserve to have a little fun every now and then."

"That's what Sloan says."

"I might like this Sloan after all."

"A boy in my math class did ask me to go to a dance," I admit.

Mom leans back and claps her hands. Mimi lets out a whoop from behind the door. Apparently I'm not the only one who eavesdrops.

"But I told him I couldn't. And now he's never going to want to go with me."

Mom squeezes my hands.

"I might have an idea, but you have to trust me. Do you trust me, Franny?"

Her hands are steady and her eyes are clear. I nod, and for this moment, at least, it's the truth.

"Good. Now you go on up and I'll be right behind you. I have a few calls to make."

"About that," I say, and fish her phone out of my backpack.

Her eyes grow wide in surprise.

"Any more secrets you'd like to get off your chest?" she asks.

I shake my head.

"Good. Now go, before I change my mind and decide to ground you."

29

APOLOGIES

I FORGOT WHAT IT WAS LIKE to be afraid to walk into math class. Today is a good reminder. As soon as I sit down, Sloan turns around and starts talking to Lacey and Rosa.

"I saw your dress for the dance on IG yesterday. That neckline is *gorgeous*," she gushes to Lacey. As if Sloan ever cared about *necklines* before.

"*Shhh*, girl! I don't want Jeremy to hear you!" Lacey shouts. She is making absolutely sure Jeremy is paying attention.

"Hey, Sloan," I whisper when she turns around. I feel pukey with nerves, but I've got to get this apology out. I stayed up half the night planning what I would say. I'll tell her the whole truth about Mom's accident and why I was cleaning those houses and I'll say sorry for the whole blackmailing thing. *Then*, if she lets me get all the way to this part, I'll offer to keep tutoring her.

But Lacey interrupts. "So who are *you* going with?"

I wait for Sloan to laugh. She was making fun of the

Spring Bash poster right along with me. But she doesn't. She tilts her head toward the classroom door, where a boy is walking in. My heart bottoms out.

"Ohh, no *way!*" Lacey squeals. "You and Noah?"

At the sound of his name, Noah looks up.

"Dude!" Jeremy yells from the back. He points at Sloan. "Niiiiiiice."

"He *never* goes to these things," Rosa whispers to her.

"Well, I guess he needed a change," Sloan says, and smirks at me.

And just like that we are back to our original positions.

"Why do you look like someone stole your last Oreo, kid?" Mimi asks when we pull up to Cheesed after school.

"You mean other than the fact that I'm about to have to *humiliate* myself in front of two people who are basically strangers in a restaurant full of people who are *definitely* strangers?"

She puts the truck in park. "Yeah, besides that."

I could lie. Tell her I have a headache or a ton of homework. But I'm sick of lying, so I stick to the truth. "I found out today that my first real friend is going to the dance with the first guy I ever liked who might have liked me back if I hadn't been such a jerk to him."

Mimi whistles. "Well, that is downright Shakespearean," she says.

I bury my head in my hands. "Yeah, well, it's my life."

"The heart will break, kid. But the broken live on." She leans over and opens my door.

I sigh and get down from the truck. "That's from AA, isn't it?" I ask.

"Nope. Lord Byron. He was a poet—and they are experts at heartbreak. Go on, now."

The inside of Cheesed is dim but cheery. The wood tables are glossy with polish, and metal buckets filled with napkins and silverware and homemade ketchup sit in the center like bouquets of flowers. A big chalkboard behind the counter displays the specials in bright blue lettering. I had no idea there were so many ways to make grilled cheese. Something called "The Elvis" has goat cheese, bananas, soy bacon, *and* peanut butter on it. That has to be a joke.

I spot Claire Kusel at the counter taking orders. Her strawberry-blond hair is braided and up in a twist like something out of *The Sound of Music*. She is chatting with a woman snuggling a baby in a sling. The woman bounces a little up and down, and Claire wiggles her fingers at the baby.

Ugh. Claire is *nice*. I bet her husband, Jason, is too, and now I've got to go introduce myself and tell her I've been taking her money and eating her cheese under false pretenses. Well, technically, Sloan ate most of the cheese.

It was almost easier with the Ellsworths because she

caught me in the act. When I went to apologize and stood on those stone steps with her looking down at me, the dislike was already written on her face. It took all of two seconds.

I told her about Mom's accident and she said, "Well, that doesn't explain why you were digging through my things." So I said, "You're right. I'm sorry." She shook her head. "I've hired a cleaning company. Tell your mother her services are no longer needed." And I said, "Okay." End of discussion.

When the woman with the baby leaves and there's no one else in line so I have no excuse not to, I drag my feet up to the counter.

"Um, are you Claire?" I ask, because I can't come right out and say, "Hey, I know you from the wedding photo on your mantel."

"Yes, I'm Claire. How can I help you?" She smiles and picks up her pad of paper to take my order. I panic.

"Umm, I'll take the Elvis with a side of seasoned fries. To go, please."

She writes it down, tears off the slip, and passes it through a window into the kitchen. Great start.

"That's a customer favorite," she says, and hands me a metal stick with the number eleven at the top. When I continue to stand there instead of walking away like a normal person, she tilts her head.

"I'm sorry. Did you want to order something else?"

She is so nice. I've got to tell her.

"No, I'm Julia's daughter. Julia Bishop?" I say, my voice going high at the end.

"Oh my goodness!" She comes around from behind the counter. "You're Franny! Your mother has said such wonderful things about you!" She looks around. "Is she here?"

"No, ma'am. It's just me." I grip my number eleven like a tiny shield. "My mom was in a car accident about six weeks ago, and she broke her femur. You know, the thigh bone." I point to my own leg as if Claire doesn't know what a femur is. *Get it together, Franny.*

Claire opens her mouth, and I can tell she's about to say she is *so sorry* and then follow it up with all these other kind words. She hasn't pieced it together yet—how her condo has been magically getting cleaned. I spit out the rest.

"Anyway, I've been the one cleaning your place, and I'm really sorry I didn't tell you and that I entered your home without your permission and took your money and also probably didn't do as good a job as Mom."

Claire's mouth hangs open. I fill the air between us with more words.

"Mom didn't find out until last night. That's why I'm here. Not that she's making me apologize. I would have come clean anyway. Ha ha, *come clean.* Sorry, that's a terrible joke. So, ummmm—"

I shut my mouth, mostly because there's nothing left to say, but also because someone is yelling "Number eleven! Number *eleven*!"

I hold up my number. A guy with a black goatee and man bun weaves his way through the tables toward me. It's Jason, holding a paper bag with *#11* on it. Of course it is.

"Babe, everything okay? There's a line," he says, and Claire and I both turn to see people standing one behind the other, almost to the door, waiting to order.

"I'm on it," Claire says, taking the bag and handing it to me. She doesn't say anything to Jason, thank goodness, who hurries back to the kitchen.

"It's on the house," she says with the kindest smile that I don't deserve. When I open the door and the bell jingles, I turn to give her a little wave on my way out, but she's busy taking orders.

It's weird, in a nice way, how some of the things I think will be big deals turn out to be not so big at all. I'm about to tell Mimi this when I get in the truck, but she's too distracted by the food in the bag.

"What'd you say is in this, again?" Mimi asks when I offer her half the sandwich.

"Peanut butter, banana, soy bacon ... I can't remember what else."

We stare through the windshield at the smiling slice of cheese over the door.

"Well," she says, wiping her fingers on a paper napkin, "congrats on making amends, Franny. This redemption is *delicious*."

When I get home, belly full of forgiveness and bacon, Meg is sitting next to Mom on Oscar, which is weird because I have literally never seen Meg sit down, ever.

"There she is!" Mom cheers, and slaps her knees.

"Uh, hi?" I say, looking from her to Meg. "Am I late for something?"

"Nope." Mom grins at Meg, and the corner of Meg's mouth twitches, her version of a smile.

Meg turns to me. "Your mom wanted to wait for you."

"Wait for me for what?"

Mom holds up a finger. "Watch and see." She grabs her rainbow crutch from the floor and stands. Meg moves in front of her with her hands out. Then Mom lets the crutch fall back on Oscar and holds her own hands just above Meg's. They look like they're about to play the hand-slapping game. Then Meg takes a step backward.

I run toward them. Meg's too far away! If Mom stumbles, she'll fall. But before I can get there, Mom is . . . Mom is stepping forward on her injured leg without hopping, without falling, without wincing in pain. Meg moves again, and I stop breathing. Mom takes another step. Without me or Meg or the crutch. Mom is walking!

186

"Check it out, kiddo. I'm doing it!" Mom shouts.

"You totally are!" I shout back, even though at this point we are only a foot away.

"She totally is," Meg says, and her face cracks into a *real* cheek-crinkling smile.

They continue their no-touching slow dance until they make a full lap around the living room and end back at me, where I am hopping in place. I throw myself at Mom in a hug, which includes Meg, too, because I am Team Meg all the way now.

Meg is the first to pull away. When she does, I swear she's blinking away some almost-tears. Not going to lie, so am I. When Mom sees us both, she pretends to wipe some sweat from her forehead and then takes a slow, deep bow.

30

A CORDIAL INVITATION

"YOU WANT ME TO WHAT?" I ask Mom on Wednesday night over bowls of ramen noodles.

"I want you to invite Noah and Sloan to the Easter play," she explains, like it's not the most terrible idea in the world.

"You have noodle juice on your chin." I hand her a napkin. "And also, no."

She puts down her spoon. "Why not? He invited *you* to something. Then you said no and basically danced all over his poor broken heart. And you still haven't told Sloan the truth about why you roped her into cleaning in the first place."

"I tried!"

"Well, this can be your chance to try again."

"But it's an *Easter* play, at *church*."

"Yes, and what better reminder of the need for forgiveness? Also, the cast will be amazingly dressed." She points to the metal clothing rack that Ruthann brought over. Thanks to Mom, it is positively bursting with Jesus apparel.

On a scale of one to ten, how humiliating would it be to

invite my ex-friend and her date, aka the boy I like, to this thing? And would it be even more humiliating if they said yes?

"I don't think I can do that."

"Of course you can," Mom says. "And really," she adds, "what have you got to lose?"

I flip through the scrapbooking paper Mom unearthed from her craft closet.

"Mom?"

"Yeah, kiddo?"

"I'm not sure I even want them there. Sloan stole Noah from me. And Noah *let* himself be stolen." Saying the words brings the ache back sharp enough to make me wince.

Mom slurps the last of her ramen straight out of the bowl and studies me.

"I get that. But this isn't really about them."

I raise my eyebrows. "It isn't?"

"Making amends isn't about the other person. Not really. It's about doing everything you can to end a hurt you caused. You ever heard the phrase 'tying up loose ends'?"

I shake my head.

"This apology is like tying off a thread. When I sew a last stitch on a project and make that knot, I can finally lay it down, because it's finished. Tying things up is meant to give you peace." She puts her hand on mine. "You can let it go after that, knowing you've done all you can."

"But what about what they did to me?"

"Well, that's the thing about people bumping up against each other in a hurting world, Franny. You can't make anybody else do the right thing. You just have to keep doing the right thing for you."

After that it's only a matter of digging deep enough into Mom's sewing closet to find what I hope I need to pull off the first step in this mega apology.

I stay up way too late working on it. I could just ask them to come to the play when I'm in class, but that would involve speaking words and then having to watch them react—two things I am totally not prepared to do.

I would never pretend to be a crafty person like Mom. But armed with scrapbooking paper, scissors, and my very best set of Sharpies, I manage to make three halfway decent formal invitations to an Easter play I don't even really want to go to. I leave one on my bed for later and put the other two in my bag.

I am so early for math that I beat Mr. Jamison into the room. I wait for him by his desk, feeling like the world's lamest teacher's pet. I owe him an apology too. So many apologies. It's exhausting and embarrassing, and also necessary.

Mr. Jamison comes in, in a hurry, followed by a trickle of students, including Noah and Sloan. I try not to think about why they are arriving together.

"Franny! Hello! Sorry, I'm a little rushed today. The copier got jammed, and someone thought it would be a fun surprise to replace all the plain paper with this." He holds up a stack of hot-pink paper. I imagine Ms. Taylor printing off thousands of Spring Bash flyers and running through the halls, tossing them in the air like Monopoly money.

"It's okay, sir. I just have one quick question and one statement."

"Okay. Hit me with the question first."

"I was hoping—well, would you mind giving me more of those advanced problems that I didn't get right the first time?"

He sets down the pile of pink and resettles his glasses on his nose.

"Franny, I love your enthusiasm . . ."

He trails off, and I wait for the "but."

"But"—there it is—"I saw how upset you got when I returned your work. I don't want you to put so much pressure on yourself."

"I won't, sir! That's why I'm here. That's the statement part: I want to apologize for how I reacted. I'm not great at hearing that I'm not great at something, but I really appreciate the time you put into making that folder for me." I give him what I hope is a winning smile. And then I circle back to my question. "Sooo, I want more problems so I can really learn. I'm not as afraid to make mistakes this time around. I think you should let me try again."

He looks at me for a very long minute.

"Okay, Franny." He holds out his hand and I shake it, because it's not embarrassing when a grown-up does it. "Let's try again."

"Excellent! Thank you!" I walk backward to my seat as fast as I can, before he changes his mind.

The atmosphere at our table is twenty degrees colder than in the rest of the room. Sloan doesn't laugh or joke with Lacey. Noah leaves his bag at his feet. They both have that glazed look where they're pretending to listen to Mr. Jamison, but I'd bet all my money that neither one could tell you a thing he said about negative numbers.

My hands are sweaty, and part of me wants to go ahead and slip the invitations to Sloan and Noah right now, in the middle of class, and get it over with. But if I do, there's a risk they'll open them and I'll have to watch. Then we'll be stuck in this row like prisoners chained together until the bell rings. I should just stick with the original plan, which is to basically lob the invites in their general direction at the end of class and flee.

I made Sloan's in the shape of a blue Nike swoosh and covered it in silver glitter. It's sparkly *and* sporty, which I thought she would appreciate. Noah's is a horrible attempt at an origami Sonic Oreo Blast with a removable spoon. There may or may not be a pun in there about how "cool" and "chill" it would be for him to come to the play. It seemed like a good idea at two in the morning, but now I wonder which would win for most embarrassing—this invite or the bend-and-snap?

One minute before class ends, I open my planner. At thirty seconds left, I slide the invitations out. When the bell rings, I push them in their direction and speed-walk out the door.

Mrs. Ivey is my last apology. So after school, Mom and I take the bus to her house. She waves at us from her spot on the couch, where she's feeding Petunia a slice of bologna and watching *Wheel of Fortune*. We settle in next to her to watch for a bit. I solve the puzzle for "Won't You Be My Neighbor." I love Mister Rogers. Mrs. Ivey doesn't ask why we're here on a Thursday or why Mom is with me.

Her not asking makes me fidgety, and I pick at the plastic covering of the couch. I'm a little worried about what the shock might do to her when I admit to everything. I don't know how old she is, but she's old enough to wobble when she stands and to use jumbo pencils on her word puzzles. Right now she smells like bologna and rose soap. I can't believe I lied to a woman who owns a kitten calendar and a poodle named Petunia.

"Mrs. Ivey?"

"Yes, Franny?" In the blue glow of the TV her skin looks so pale you can see the tiny veins underneath. This is going to kill her.

"How're you feeling today?"

She clicks the TV off and turns the full force of her bifocals on me.

"I know you didn't come all the way here to ask about my health."

Mom nudges my knee with hers. It's both reassuring and a *get on with it* gesture.

Here goes nothing.

"Okay. So, truth is, Mom isn't helping Mimi remodel the laundromat. Six weeks ago Mom got injured in a car accident. It wasn't her fault. But she couldn't work, and so I decided to do it for her without telling her . . . or you. I'm sorry I took your money. And I'm sorry for keeping it a secret."

She blinks once at me with her watery eyes.

"Honey," she says finally, "tell me something I don't know."

Say what?

"You knew?"

"Of course I knew. You don't live as many years as I have in a town as small as this one without keeping track of your neighbors."

She pats Petunia, who shakes with delight.

"My niece works triage at Memorial West."

"You knew *from the very beginning*," I say, disbelieving.

"I did. But you seemed so determined with your fixer-upper story. Going on and on about paint colors and retil-ing—"

Mom snorts and I elbow her.

"I figured you had your reasons for keeping it quiet."

All along I thought I was so smart, fooling Mrs. Ivey, and she was fooling me right back. I've been conned by a little old lady.

"So why'd you let me keep coming?"

"Well, dear, I still needed the house cleaned."

"I really am sorry I lied to you."

She waves her hand in the air. "All's forgiven."

I hug her gently over Petunia's head and then fish out the third and final invitation from my bag. It's a drawing of a purple trumpet-shaped flower. I had to look it up on the internet. I hope it's right.

"A petunia for Petunia!" She beams and fumbles to open it. Mom leans over me to help.

"I figured you might need something to do tomorrow . . . on *Good Friday*," I add with emphasis even though I'm tech-nically not supposed to know it's her dead husband's birthday.

She reads out loud:

"Dear Mrs. Alma Ivey,
You are cordially invited to the Pageant Wagon's
Easter Jubilee.
Location: Cedarville Presbyterian

Transportation: provided
Attire: whatever you want
Sincerely,
Frances Bishop"

She'll probably say no. She never leaves the house.

"Well," she says after a minute, "I guess I'm going to have to dig out my church clothes."

Wow. Mrs. Ivey is full of surprises.

"Oh, I can most certainly help with that!" Mom offers.

"Also," I add, "I'd like to keep coming by, if that's all right. Not for pay or anything. Just to visit. Petunia's still going to need walking."

She blows her nose and pats me on the knee. Mom warned me that just because someone gets older and needs more help, it doesn't mean they lose their pride. It can be hard to let other people do something for you if you feel like it's a favor. I don't think that's particular to senior citizens. Nobody likes to ask for help. I brace for rejection.

But she says, "That'd be nice," and turns *Wheel of Fortune* back on so we can watch the lightning round.

31

WATCHING THE CLOCK

FRIDAY, APRIL 16

NO SCHOOL

Help Mimi set up Easter display

Only check the clock ~~once~~ twice an hour

6:30 p.m.—Pick up Mrs. Ivey

6:45 p.m.—Arrive at Cedarville Presbyterian

7:00 p.m.—The Pageant Wagon's Easter Jubilee

I WAKE UP FRIDAY MORNING with a stomach full of gravel. No one has my number. I have no way of knowing if Sloan or Noah will show until we actually pull up in front of the church tonight. I roll over and stare at the paper bird and turtle and fox on my windowsill. The rose has its own place of prominence in the needle box on my dresser. I have twelve long hours to fill before the suspense is over.

Never have I ever wanted to go to school more. At school, time is neatly marked in class-sized increments. It ticks by as expected, and whether you like it or not, something new starts every forty-five to forty-eight minutes. But today time just drags, like the earth needs a new battery. Right now, everyone is home, sleeping in and binge-watching superhero movies on Netflix. We don't even own a TV.

I sit up and pull out the new math folder that Mr. Jamison gave me. It's green. I spread it open on my bed along with pencils, a calculator, and lined paper in case I need extra space to work out the problems. I experiment with pacing myself, skipping parts I don't understand and making notes to the side with little question marks so I can ask him later. It's a new way to work. I don't totally love it. Those big gaps are like bug bites I can't scratch. Makes me itchy just looking at them.

By nine, even math isn't distracting enough. I'm jumpy and bored at the same time. My brain keeps glitching like a bad internet connection. Also, the whirring of Mom's sewing machine has gotten so loud, it's burrowing into my skull. I swear she turbo-charged it.

I take my sweet time getting dressed, because what else do I have to do, and then venture into the living room. Mom's bent over the light blue Singer, her hair tucked under a red paisley bandana. The Singer is the one item in our house we bought new. We visited Jo-Ann's craft store every week for months, waiting for it to go on sale. When she finally bought it, Mom called it a "work investment" and christened it Layla.

From the sound of it, Layla is in a mood today. I don't know if you can overwork a machine, but Mom is sure testing the limits. On the floor at her feet sit three disciples' cloaks, Mary Magdalene's bright blue head covering, and some swathes of red velvet on their way to becoming tunics for the Roman soldiers.

"How's things?" I ask.

Mom jumps and her foot slips off the pedal. The sewing machine slows to a halt. *You owe me one, Layla.*

"*Goodgoodgood!* We're all good!" She's talking at warp speed, and her left eyelid is twitching. Oh boy.

"Why don't you take a break?"

"Can't! I have to get these to the church by two."

Mom seems worried? Excited? I can't tell. I've never seen this expression on her face. It hits me for the first time that this is a big deal for her. She's been selling her creations on Etsy for years, but this is an entire production. Every single person onstage will be wearing what *she* put together, and everyone in the audience will see it and like it . . . or not.

"Hey, Mom."

"Yeah, kiddo?"

I don't know what to say. How do you tell your parent you're proud of them?

"I like the gold trim on the soldiers' skirts."

"Ha! I think they're technically called pteruges, but thank you."

"Wow. You did your research. Good, uh, job. It all looks really . . . biblical."

"Well, let's hope so."

She straightens and pops her back, which I've told her a million times not to do. Then she blows me an air kiss. "Back to it! Can you pass me that cup of coffee?"

"I don't think caffeine is the answer," I say, but do it anyway.

She takes a sip and pauses long enough to eye me over her cup. "You nervous about tonight?"

I hold up a hand. "We are *not* going to talk about it."

She raises her eyebrows and starts to open her mouth.

"You know what?" I say. "You're right. You should get back to work. I'll go downstairs and see if Mimi needs help with the window display."

I grab a granola bar and make a hasty exit.

Downstairs, the laundromat is packed. Everyone is taking advantage of the long weekend to get their washing done. I don't even want to guess how many bunny- and chick-covered church dresses are running through the delicate cycle right now.

Mimi spots me from her perch on a stepstool by the big window that overlooks the street.

"Pass me that decal," she shouts over the hum of all ten dryers running at the same time.

I unpeel a three-foot carrot from its plastic backing and

carry it over to her as carefully as I can. She already has the bunny in place. Its giant toothy face creeps me out, but the kids seem to like it. I watch as she smooths the carrot onto the window, running the flat side of a knife across the back to get out all the air bubbles.

"Need help?"

Her overalls are rolled up to the knee. Even with the door propped open, it's one thousand degrees in here from the heat of the dryers.

"I got this. You do the eggs, if we can distract the kids long enough for you to hide them."

She points to the garbage bag overflowing with plastic Easter eggs that we filled with jelly beans last night. We hide them on the small patch of lawn outside the laundromat. Last year, the parents were so grateful for the ten minutes of peace without their kids that they set up a tip jar. We labeled it $ FOR THE EASTER BUNNY and left it by the vending machines. It's been there all year.

I spend the next few hours hiding eggs and then refilling them and hiding them again for the next round of customers. That gets me to lunch. If I survive the wait, the pageant part of today will be easy.

At noon, I walk into town and buy us all sandwiches from Cheesed. They are way beyond our budget, but I can't stop thinking about that Elvis sandwich. Claire is there, and so is Jason. She must have filled him in, because when my order is up, he comes out from the kitchen and hands it to me without hurrying away.

"Nice to officially meet you," he says.

I blush and say, "Same," because it's never not going to be weird that I know he sleeps on the left side of the bed and owns beard oil that smells like pine sap.

At a quarter to two, Mimi and Mom and I load all the costumes, wrapped carefully in garment bags, into the back of the pickup. We drive over to the church. Ruthann and some other ladies stand at the tailgate like band groupies while Mom passes it all down. I catch Mimi watching them out of the rearview mirror.

"You're not going to get out and say hello?" I tease.

Mimi clucks her tongue. "That woman doesn't need a hello from me. She needs a nap and a new hair color."

"*Ohhh*, I thought you weren't supposed to judge."

Right then, Derek comes out the back doors of the church rolling a black partition.

"What's *he* doing here?"

"*He* is helping set the stage tonight for the show," Mimi answers. "They needed an extra hand, and I suggested he apply."

I watch him walk across the pavement toward Mom. He helps her unload the last few bags.

"You sure he's reliable?" I cross my arms.

Mimi turns to me. "Look who's judging now, Miss High and Mighty."

"I'm just saying, he quit AA. What makes you think he won't quit this?"

Mimi narrows her eyes. "And how would *you* know about that? I thought my meetings were *anonymous*."

Whoops.

We both face forward again, and Mimi adjusts her mirror and sighs.

"We've got to keep giving people grace, Franny. Even when they don't deserve it. *Especially* when they don't deserve it."

Ruthann laughs at something Mom says, and Mimi frowns like she got a bad taste in her mouth.

"You were saying?" I ask.

She flips on the radio and pretends not to hear me.

At 6:30 on the dot, I lead Mrs. Ivey to the truck. She totters on white low-heeled shoes.

"Don't you look lovely!" Mom exclaims like she's surprised, even though she's the one who helped pick out the lavender jacket and skirt.

"It's not polite to lie to an old lady," Mrs. Ivey says, but she touches the white hat pinned to her hair and smiles.

We park in the back, next to the dumpster, because Ruthann sent Mom an emergency text that none of the "crowd of witnesses" knows how to fasten their robes and they need her help ASAP in the Sunday-school corridor.

Mimi and I escort Mrs. Ivey to the sanctuary and get her settled in the front row, where Mom made us *swear* to save seats. She wants to take pictures of all her costumes in action. Mimi said she'd rather spend the evening watching the dumpster than watching Ruthann, but she spread programs over six folding chairs anyway.

I'd like to hide by the trash myself, but that's not an option. There's nothing for me to do but go out front and wait. I thought we'd be early, but people are coming up the steps in droves. They are wearing everything from their Sunday best to T-shirts and flip-flops. One guy tries to enter without a shirt. I'm glad Mom made me put on my blue sundress. It's the nicest thing I own and the least ruffly, even though it's one size too small.

Then, over the next twenty minutes, everything happens exactly as I imagined it would. I sit. Strangers enter. Time passes. My stomach clenches and unclenches. The crowd slows to a trickle, until there's no hope and I'm worn out from wishing. I don't need to check my watch to know that it's over. Sloan and Noah aren't coming.

I get up, straighten the straps on my dress, and go back in. I should be happy they didn't show, right? I made my amends, like Mom said. My part is done. Now they can live happily ever after together. I don't even *want* to see them here.

32

PAGEANTRY

THE CHURCH CARRIES THE HEADACHY scent of lilies and candles and floor wax. As the lights dim, I stop halfway down the aisle. I'll hide in the lobby. It's better than sitting next to two empty seats.

I turn around. The doors are still open, and the early-evening twilight is just begging for me to escape. Then I remember Mom double- and triple-checking all the garment bags, the iron, the cordless steamer. This is important to her. I turn and drag my feet back down the musty carpet.

One, two, three, four . . . nine steps to our row, and there's nothing to do but sit in the loser seat. Five heads turn my way. Wait, five? I freeze at the end of the aisle, because my brain short-circuits at the math.

Sloan and Noah are *here*.

"Uh," I say eloquently.

Mom waves her program from the farthest seat. She winks oh-so-subtly.

"Hi," Noah says, and gets up to let me sit between him and Sloan.

"Hi," I say, and sit, because it's the only thing to do.

He is wearing a light blue button-down shirt and khakis and shoes that have for sure been polished. I can't look at him longer than a few seconds.

"We came in the side door," Sloan explains, casual as always in her T-shirt and cropped leggings.

My brain gets stuck on the word "we" and wondering if they came together and if this is a date and how awkward is it that I am now sitting in between them?

"Oh. Okay."

I fold my hands in my lap. We are finally in the configuration I wasn't brave enough to pull off in math class—me in the middle. I want to slip through the cracks like a puddle.

"I liked your invitation," Noah leans over and whispers.

"Ditto," Sloan adds, and then shoulder-bumps me. "Although I think I should have gotten the Sonic one." What happened to make them be so nice to me? Is this a prank? Are they texting each other right now on the sly about how hilarious this all is? What a great story for Lacey and Rosa and the guys on the basketball team on Monday. My armpits start to sweat as Pastor Carl walks onstage in full Jesus dress and holds up his hands for everybody to be quiet.

"Ladies and gentlemen," he booms. "We are happy to open our doors and our hearts tonight for an *extra-special* performance by the Pageant Wagon on what we in the church consider the most im-*por*-tant weekend of the year!"

It's hard to take him seriously. With his bald head and that long flowing robe, he looks like a giant baby in a nightgown.

"We welcome the chance to bring this most important message of hope to our regular church folk and to visitors both new and long-absent." He holds out his arms and his sleeves billow.

Down the row, Mimi snorts so loudly that Pastor Carl turns his head toward her. It is definitely *not* my imagination that his face turns red under the spotlight.

"Now, uh, without, uh—"

"It seems Pastor Carl has lost the *most important message*," Sloan whispers, and Noah laughs. I try to, but it gets stuck in my throat because I'm not sure they're laughing with me or at me for inviting them to this.

Meanwhile, Mrs. Ivey cups her hand to her ear and yells, "Speak up, Carl! We can't hear you!"

Pastor Carl clears his throat and turns away from our row when he says, "Without further ado, 'The Easter Jubilee: A Message of Hope'!"

The next sixty minutes are entertaining enough to almost make me forget Sloan and Noah. Almost.

Ruthann is a fiery Mary Magdalene. She outshines Peter and the angel when she yells at the edge of the cardboard tomb, "They have taken the Lord and we don't know where they put him!"

"She's got some lungs on her, doesn't she?" Mrs. Ivey comments, and fans herself with her program.

Then Carl comes out dressed in rags as the risen Jesus and barks, "*Woman*, why are you crying?"

Mimi mutters, "*Of course* he made himself the son of God." Mom swats her arm and takes a picture with her phone.

Toward the end, Ruthann trips on her headpiece while hurrying to the disciples. For a second it looks like she's about to knock them down like bowling pins. But Derek races out from the wings wearing all black and catches her by the elbow. He slips back behind the cardboard tomb when Ruthann steadies herself and shouts "I have seen the Lord!" loud enough to hear from the street.

"Well, this is action-packed," Noah whispers to me, and he smells like Dial soap and sunshine and I don't hear anything else after that.

After a few hymns and the waving of palm branches and lilies, the Pageant Wagon players bow to enthusiastic applause and cheers. With the lights up again, you can really see how great a job Mom did on all the costumes. Each detail is perfect.

"That. Was. Everything," Sloan says, and leans back against her seat. There is no curtain to close, so the actors walk straight down the steps off the stage to mingle with the crowd. I study her as she watches them. My chest rises with hope. I think she really means it.

Grinning, Noah leans over to say, "Really, Franny, that was awesome." I'm so light, I could lift off the ground. Then he adds, "We're so glad you invited us," and I sink right back down. There it is, the "we" and "us." The one-two punch. It's not a prank. It's pity. They came together because they felt sorry for me. I nod and smile and hold it until my cheeks hurt.

Mom half walks, half dances up to us and throws her arms around me.

"Marvelous, right?" she laughs into my hair. "Who wouldn't have a come-to-Jesus moment after seeing those disciples' robes?" I hold on tight when she starts to pull away. I need a minute to collect myself.

"Mom, it was a thing of beauty," I say when I finally let her go. "Layla would be proud."

"The old girl did well, didn't she?" Mom grins from me to Sloan to Noah. "You must be Franny's friends. Nice to finally meet you both!" She releases me to shake their hands. I still can't look at them, and I'm saved from full-on introductions by Ruthann, who rushes up with a huge bundle of sunflowers for Mom.

"Thank you, my dear. You *made* the show!" she gushes. There is a dark line of foundation along her jaw, and her eyebrows are drawn high in permanent surprise. She looks frightening up close. But also kind of beautiful. That hair was made for the stage.

Mom blushes and hugs the flowers like a kid.

"So I was talking with the other players," Ruthann says, beaming at Mom.

"The who?" I ask.

"The *players*, dear, the *actors*. They want to hire your mother to make *all* their costumes. If she's up for it?" Ruthann arches an eyebrow—the real one, which is miles below the penciled one.

"You want me to make all the outfits for the Pageant Wagon?" Mom asks.

Ruthann lets out a bark of a laugh. "Oh no, Julia. Not *this*. We want you for the community theater. We do six plays a year, and we have annual subscribers and a real budget, which means we could pay you! It's not much, but we would love to have you."

Mom opens her mouth and closes it and opens it again. She looks at me and then down at the flowers and then back at Ruthann. She's never been at a loss for words—that's my thing. I give her a nudge with my shoulder.

"Oh. Yes. Yes, *of course*."

"Excellent," Ruthann says with a nod that is all business. Then Mimi appears.

"Mimi," I say, moving in between her and Ruthann. "Ruthann just offered Mom a job making costumes for the community theater. A *paying* job. Isn't that great?"

Mimi looks over my head at Mom, who is grinning so wide, her eyes are all scrunched up. Then she turns to Ruthann.

They stare at each other long enough for Mom to clear her throat and pull me back, just in case. Off to the side, Sloan and Noah are laughing at something I can't hear. I lean into Mom a little more.

Ruthann blinks first and Mimi nods. "Well, okay," she says. And then, to everyone's total shock, Mimi adds, "You had some good moments up there."

"Thank you." Ruthann stands taller than I've ever seen her.

"Much better than that old man." Mimi tips her head toward Pastor Carl, who is mopping sweat off his shiny forehead with the sleeve of his nightgown-slash-Jesus robe.

Ruthann pauses, and we all hold our breath again to see if she's going to bawl Mimi out for disrespecting her pastor. Then she busts out a belly-shaking laugh. Mimi claps her on the back and joins in. It is an Easter miracle.

Behind them, I spot Derek on the stage beginning to disassemble the tomb, his blond hair plastered to his forehead with sweat. It must be hot under those lights. He catches me watching, and after a second or two, I lift my hand and wave. He gives me a "what's up" chin nod, and we both pause long enough to make me walk over.

"Hey, Derek. Good job on the sets." Lame. But true. The church ladies sure aren't up to the heavy lifting.

He sits down on the stage stairs so I don't have to look up at him. When we're level, though, I can't meet his gaze.

I'm embarrassed about the note. I shouldn't have told him to stay away. Mom was right. We all deserve as many second chances as we can get.

"Franny," he says in a low whisper.

"Yeah."

"I know you said no amends, but—"

I glance at him.

"This goes without saying, but drugs make people do stupid things."

No kidding.

"So, anyway." He runs his hand through his hair, spiking it up again. "I'm not real good with words, so I'll keep it short. That night at your mom's was rock bottom for me. I'm—" He looks away. "I'm embarrassed. And I'm sorry. I'm trying to do . . . better."

He sits back, worn out now. I get it. Apologies are exhausting.

It feels weird to be on the other side of sorry. I don't really know what to say, but I don't think he expects anything. I kind of nod at him, and he gives me a nod in return. Then he stands to get back to work. And that's that. I wish every apology could be that simple.

When I return to the front row, the crowd has already begun to thin. Mimi walks Mrs. Ivey down the aisle while Mom heads out to load up the truck. Before I can offer to help anyone, they all abandon me, and I'm left alone with

Sloan and Noah. I turn around, half expecting them to be holding hands under a bouquet of lilies, but Noah's on his phone and Sloan is shredding the leaves off a palm frond.

"No reception," he says, before I can figure out what to say or how to say it. "I'm going outside to call my mom to pick me up." He's walking up the aisle when it finally registers that he *didn't* come with Sloan and now I've missed my chance to give him the whole speech I had prepared. *I'm sorry for freaking out on you and thank you for the animals and can we please still be friends?* I shout in my head toward his back, for all the good it does me.

There's still one person standing next to me who I also owe some words. She's winnowed her palm frond down to a pointy sword and looks like she knows how to use it.

"Sloan—" I begin. She swishes her palm sword at me, and I can't tell if she's playing. "I'm really, really sorry for everything that went down at Mrs. Ellsworth's. I'm sorry I got mad at you about the pills and . . ."

Sloan drops the palm sword and crosses her arms. "You were mad at me before that."

"I know. I'm sorry. I was a jerk. It wasn't about you. There's a lot I haven't told you. . . ." How much do I tell her about my mom and our past and why I was really cleaning the houses? If truth is a pie, how big a slice can she handle?

She holds up her hand. "Stop."

"But I really need to—"

"No, Franny, you don't! Geez, you're pushy." Sloan lets out a huff, then narrows her eyes at me. "Mrs. Ivey called my house last night."

"She *did*?"

"Technically, I'm grounded, so no phone, but since Mrs. Ivey is an old lady, Mom figured it was okay."

"Ummm, what'd she say?" I can't even picture it—Mrs. Ivey calling the Tates and asking to speak to Sloan.

Sloan shifts from foot to foot and doesn't look at me. Oh. She knows *everything* now. Mrs. Ivey should have just minded her own business.

"Forget it. I'll just go." The door is twenty steps from here. I can make it out in five seconds at a run.

"Wait." Sloan grabs my arm. "I'm sorry."

I turn back, because her grip's pretty good, and also, *what*?

"Mrs. Ivey explained about your mom's accident and how you were hard up for cash. You know," she adds, "you could have told me."

"Yeah, that would have gone over well. How many times would you have kicked my bag across the classroom for that?"

She pulls at a loose thread from her leggings.

"I was kind of terrible to you, huh?"

"Pretty much, but I guess I was asking for it with the homemade clothes and frizzy hair."

Sloan shakes her head. "You weren't asking for it. And it wasn't your clothes or your hair. I just—"

"You just what?"

"You always seemed like you knew what you were doing, and you were *so* serious and smart and exactly the kind of person my dad . . ." She throws her hands up in the air. "Never mind. It was frustrating, I guess."

It's strange to hear someone describe you to yourself. She makes me sound intimidating, which is hilarious, considering she's the one with the sharp elbows.

"I'm sorry," I say.

"*Don't* apologize for having it together."

"But I don't! I really, *really* don't. I fell apart when the plan fell apart. I'm a total mess."

She gives me an *are you serious* once-over. "Well, we can be messes together." Then she suddenly finds something very interesting to study on the floor. "And about the whole Noah thing . . . I shouldn't have done that. That was . . . not cool."

I think that's as close as I'm going to get to an apology from her for asking Noah to the dance. But I'll take it.

I punch her in the shoulder, and she looks up in surprise. I tip my head toward the exit sign. "Come on. Race you to the exit?"

Boy, does it feel good to stop talking and *run*. We burst through the church doors out into the night air. It smells like warm pavement and fresh-cut grass. I'm so relieved Sloan and I are okay, I could run all the way home. We are out of breath and laughing when I see him.

Noah is here. Still. He's leaning against the railing of the steps and looking right at me. All the air rushes out of my lungs. Sloan sees him eyeing me and smacks her forehead. "Oops. Forgot my phone! BRB!" She darts back inside, leaving me and Noah alone on the church steps.

"Uh—" I stare at the front of his shirt.

"So—" he says.

I swallow and say something that's not quite the truth, but also not quite a lie.

"I'm really glad you're going to the dance with Sloan. She's awesome! I think you'll have fun!"

I force my mouth to close before I can wish them a long and happy life together.

"Franny—" he says, shaking his head. "Sloan and I aren't going to the dance together."

What? Stupid hope won't stay down. It bubbles up and up until "Why not?" pops out.

"I was bummed you and I weren't going," he says, meeting my eyes for the first time. "I was really nervous to ask you, and I had already told my moms I was going and they got way too excited and then you said no, so when Sloan asked . . . I said yes."

He didn't think I wasn't good enough for him? He

wasn't going with Sloan just to get back at me? Can you make a mental note to get out of your own head, or does that defeat the purpose?

"But you never get nervous," I say.

"Franny." He stares at me. "Come on."

"What?"

"I get nervous around you!"

This is . . . new.

"You do?"

"Yes!"

"But all the animals you gave me—the origami. You never care if the guys make fun of you for it."

"I'm a Black kid with two moms in a town that is ninety-nine point nine percent white and straight. I can't *afford* to care. I gave you the animals because I think they're cool, but also because . . . it's easier than speaking."

Oh. That last part, I get.

He backs down one step so I'm taller.

"Look, I liked you and I thought you liked me too, but then it seemed like you didn't, so—" He takes another step. He's backing away.

"I did! I mean, I do . . . like you."

"You do?" He rubs his hands over his head like he's trying to put things back into place.

My face is hot and my hands are cold and this is *way too many* conversations about feelings for one night. I nod.

"That's what Sloan said."

"She *did*?"

"Yeah. She called me this morning and told me that she thought you might like me and I should ask you again."

"Oh *really*." Old ladies *and* Sloan need to mind their own business.

"Yeah. So?" he asks, dropping his hands from his head to his pockets. "Will you go to the Spring Bash with me?"

I love Sloan. She can butt in anytime.

I must make some sort of sound that means yes, because Noah starts nodding and saying, "Okayokayokayawesome-okay."

Sloan picks that very second to return, which makes me think she was hiding behind the church doors and listening the whole time. She glances from me to Noah.

"We all sorted?" she asks.

I punch her in the arm and grin.

33

PERFECTION

SATURDAY, MAY 1

7:00 a.m.—Help Mimi open the laundromat

Noon—Drop off groceries at Mrs. Ivey's and walk
Petunia

4:00 p.m.—Go to Sloan's to get ready for
the dance! (Bring extra shoes, toothbrush,
DEODORANT)

"PLEASE TELL ME YOU'RE KIDDING."

"What?"

"You did *not* bring your math homework to my house while we are supposed to be getting ready for the dance."

I close the green folder and sit up on Sloan's giant fluffy bed.

"Don't judge me for my interests, Dreamhouse Barbie."

I wave my hand around her room. Everything is white and lacy and the exact opposite of what I would have pictured for her. I feel like I am sitting in the center of a cupcake.

She falls onto the bed next to me. The comforter is so poufy, it lets out a little whoosh.

"My dad likes nice things and I don't care, so here we are."

"Does he hate me?" I figure the fact that I tricked his daughter into becoming a maid maybe wasn't the best selling point for a new friend.

"No." Sloan kicks my leg. "He was too busy telling my mom she needed to get our household under control—'household' meaning me, I guess." We sit with that for a minute before she adds, "When I told him you were tutoring me, he said, 'That's more than your mother can do.'"

I put a hand on her arm. She leans back on an enormous heart-shaped pillow, and my hand falls away.

"Are they letting you go to gym camp?"

"Yeah, if you do a good enough job teaching me integers."

"So, no pressure."

"None whatsoever."

She sits up, and her foot knocks my folder onto the floor. It takes everything in me not to lean over and check that it's not creased. I'm working on my chill factor. I'd say I'm down from a ten to a nine point five on the worry scale.

"We have one hour to get ready for the *bash*," I inform her.

She throws a pillow at me.

"All right, all right, let's get beautiful."

We climb off the bed, which is harder than it sounds—the soft weight of it sucks you back in like the tide. I retrieve the folder. It's fine. Then I pull my dress off the hanger and hold it up to myself in front of her floor-length mirror.

When we got home the night of the play and I told Mom that Noah had asked me again, she tap-danced around the kitchen with her crutch, which she doesn't need but now uses as a prop. It was ten minutes before I could stop her.

"What am I supposed to wear?" I asked when she finally wore herself out.

"Remember when I said I had a plan?"

"Yeah."

"Well, it involves your wardrobe."

Every atom in me froze. Lace. Sequins. Plaid patches. T-shirts with snap-on collars. Corduroy pants with ruffled bottoms. I never complained about all the clothes she crafted together and bedazzled, because it made her happy to be able to do something for me. But just this once, I really, *really* wanted to look like *me* at the dance.

I thought I was doing a pretty good job of keeping my face neutral, until she asked, "What?" and followed it with, "Don't judge before you've even seen it!"

She disappeared into her bedroom to fetch "the dress." You know when a moth gets trapped under a lampshade and its wings beat frantically trying to find a way out? That's what it felt like while I sat on Oscar and waited for her to return.

When she came back in, waving a garment bag back and forth in front of her like a matador's cape, I wanted to crawl under the couch. *Please oh please don't let there be taffeta involved. Or worse,* spandex.

Then she unzipped it.

My dress is the color of the almost-night sky, so dark a blue you'd almost mistake it for black. It's sleeveless and falls just above my knees. If you look real close, the fabric shimmers, and there's a teensy wave to the bottom so that it flares out when I turn.

It's perfect.

When Sloan and I get out of her mom's car in front of the middle school, I stand up tall. It's not so much about feeling beautiful, even though I do. It's about knowing that this dress looks like *me*. I don't know how Mom did it, but for the first time, I feel like my outsides match my insides.

Sloan spots Logan and she squeals like a cheerleader, which I keep forgetting she is. Logan is on the travel gym team with Sloan, but he goes to a different school. Apparently they made a pact to be dates to each other's dances so they'd, and I quote, "have somebody who knows how to *move*." They hug and then do some sort of complicated hand-slapping routine that takes a full two minutes. Sloan insisted on wearing ballerina flats with her dress even though her mom offered her twenty bucks to wear heels.

They are still smacking each other's hands when Noah arrives. Both his moms smile and wave through the windshield of their Subaru. I wave and smile back. And then they keep waving and smiling and leaning out the window to take pictures until Noah shoos them away. I sneak a glance at him. He's wearing a black button-down shirt and dark jeans. I thought he looked good at the Easter play. This is something else. My eyes drop all the way down to his feet. Bright yellow Nikes. A laugh bursts out of me before I can catch it.

"What?" He sees me eyeing his shoes. "You want to dance, you have to come pre*pared*," he says, and does a truly terrible move he claims he learned on TikTok.

"Well, do *I* look prepared?"

I hold my hands out and spin so he can get the fully flared effect.

Noah swallows. "You look more than prepared."

My pulse ticks up. *Easy, Franny. Remember the chill factor.*

I glance over at Sloan to give myself a chance to breathe. Logan is bending her backward into an impossible shape that goes so low it turns into a backbend.

If we never set foot in the balloon-covered gym, I wouldn't care. This is already the best night I've ever had.

"Close your eyes and hold out your hand," Noah says, and I do, trying to keep it steady. He slips something onto my wrist. "Okay. Open."

It's a corsage, except not like the ones you see in movies.

A white paper rose sits in the middle of a bed of tiny dark blue paper violets. It's light as air and so beautiful I'm afraid to move.

"I called Sloan to see what color your dress was," he explains.

"I love it," I say, because I really do. But then I realize we have to go in and do the actual dancing part of the dance now, and I lose all my chill.

I look toward the road. Could I jump into one of those cars? Hitch a ride back to the laundromat with one of the parents? Noah sees it happening—my not-so-subtle freak-out. He flashes me a quick smile and holds out his arm. I force myself to take it, careful not to bend the paper flowers. Before I know it, Sloan latches on to my other arm and drags Logan into it too. This is how we enter the dance, a daisy chain of people.

"Come on, y'all," Sloan cheers when the doors open and the thrum of the bass spills out into the night. "Let's bash the heck out of this dance!"

34

THE REST OF THE STORY

I WAVE GOODBYE TO SLOAN and her mom from underneath the neon glow of MIMI'S LAUNDROMAT. A gush of warm night air follows me inside as I race up the stairs.

Wait till Mom hears all about Noah trying to teach me his terrible TikTok moves. And how Sloan landed with a *thwap* on the gym floor after Logan flipped her over his arm, swing-dance-style, and then dropped her. And how the DJ was like forty-five and kept trying to get the crowd to beat-box with him. But how none of us cared, so we ignored him and danced anyway.

Burritos would be good right now. I was too nervous to eat before we left, and we have no food in our fridge unless I want a pickle and mayonnaise sandwich, which I do not.

The drawer sticks when I yank it open. Where is the Baja's menu? And why do we have so many duck sauce pouches? I reach all the way to the back. Still no menu. I freeze. No menu and no pill bottle. I panic and pull. The drawer crashes to the ground and the corner splinters. Everything goes flying—

menus for Chinese and Mexican and hot chicken, paper napkins and plastic forks, old packets of salt and pepper, four pens with no caps. I feel sick. The pills are gone.

Blood rushes from my head so fast, everything goes black. I grab on to the counter and blink until I can see again. Mom! Where is Mom?

I flip on every single light. But I'm chasing shadows. Mom's bedroom is empty, and so is mine. The bathroom. Of course! She's probably taking a bath and listening to her CD player like last time. But it's empty too.

My legs give out, and before I can catch myself I'm on the ground. Grit from the wood floor digs into my knees. There's so much clutter—rolls of fabric and extra costumes and boxes of thread and my school bag and sneakers. But no pill bottle and no Mom.

She's really not here.

She's taken the pills and now she's passed out somewhere like Derek, except she's got no one with her, so when she stops breathing there'll be no one there to save her. I heave a couple of times, but nothing comes out. My stomach is empty and so is my mind. I don't know what to do.

"Mom!" I scream. It bounces around and echoes off the walls. This is my fault. I left her alone to go out with my friends because everyone keeps telling me to "have fun." But this is what happens when I stop taking care of us. Everything falls apart.

I crawl across the floor and grab the doorknob to pull myself up. I'll find Mimi. She can call 911 or report Mom missing to the cops, whatever she has to do. I turn back for one more look, and a slight breeze blows the sweaty hair off my face. Where's it coming from? I let go of the doorknob and walk to the row of windows. One is open. The one that leads up to the roof.

It takes a minute to shove the window all the way up. It sticks when the weather gets warmer. I haven't been up there in months. Not since before Mom's accident. I take the ladder slowly, one rung at a time, breathing in for four and out for four, because when I get to the top, Mom will either be there, or she won't. And I'm afraid to know which.

Mom sits in one of the ratty lawn chairs wearing her favorite daisy-covered dress. Her feet are on the ledge, and beside her are two glasses of lemonade in mason jars and a box tied with string. Bright red sunglasses hold back her hair. The sun's been down for hours.

I take a step. The gravel crunches. She turns toward me, a smile on her face. She's *smiling*.

She hops out of her chair and shimmies my way, her dress swaying. I back up. She stumbled a little. I saw it.

"Franny, what's wrong?"

I shake my head.

"Franny, what is it? Did something happen at the dance?"

It's too dark to check her pupils.

"Frances, talk to me!" she yells. She grabs my shoulders and starts to say more, but it's all static. *We have a bad connection*, I think, and start to laugh. It comes out in hiccups and sobs. She holds a hand to my face. I shake myself loose.

Crickets chirp in the grass below. A car alarm starts up and then is quickly silenced. I swallow. My throat hurts from all the yelling and crying.

Finally I collapse on a lawn chair. When Mom gets to me, she takes my chin in her fingers and forces me to look at her.

"Franny, you have to speak to me. Right this *minute*."

Her hands are warm.

"Where are the pills?" It hurts to speak. It hurts to ask.

She kneels at my feet in the gravelly tar.

"What pills?"

"Don't lie to me!" I scream.

"I'm not, Franny," she says slowly. "Do you mean the pills from the hospital?"

She sits on the ground. Her dress is going to be black on the bottom. "Honey, I threw them away a week ago."

She's said that before.

"How do I know you're telling the truth?"

"You can ask Mimi. I found them in the drawer when I was looking for the kitchen scissors. I called Mimi immediately. We flushed them together."

The panic leaks out slowly like spilled glue. I go limp and sink out of my chair and into her lap. She rocks me like I'm still a baby, but I don't care. I am boneless with relief. She cries and whispers into my hair, "I am so sorry. I'm so sorry," over and over again.

"It's my fault," I say when I can speak again. "I should have trusted you. I'm sorry." I start to pull away.

"No." She grips me harder. "You do *not* apologize to me."

I nod, and we both get ourselves up off the gravel and into the chairs.

I run my hands down the bottom of the beautiful dress she made me, pressing into the wrinkles that are sticky with tar. "I didn't believe you. And you've done everything right this time."

"Honey, after all I have put you through, I don't expect you to believe me. It's my job to *prove* it to you every day. That's on *me*. Not on you."

"But—"

"No buts. I have no right to ask for your faith in me. I gave that up years ago. But it is a pleasure—" She puts both hands over mine and really loses it, crying so hard her nose starts running, but she still won't let me go. "It is my *pleasure* to wake up every morning and show you that I've changed."

"I thought you took the pills because I'd left you alone."

"No, Franny! I want you to live your life and have fun with your friends. It is *not your job* to take care of me."

"But it is!"

She shakes her head. "We may have gotten things flip-flopped in the past, and that's my fault. But I am your mother. I gave birth to you and raised you, and in the order of what came first, it was me, then you, kid. You have to let me do the raising now."

She puts my hand over her heart and looks toward the sky.

"I hereby swear that Frances Bishop is absolved of all parent-related responsibilities from here on out."

We laugh, but it's tired-sounding.

"I'm no good at the kid stuff," I say, and hold out the napkin that was under her lemonade jar so she can wipe her nose.

"But you had fun tonight, right?"

I think of Noah's hand on my back as we walked out to dance and Sloan's ponytail bouncing and the sound of sneakers on the gym floor.

"I did."

"Well, then," she says, taking the napkin and passing me the lemonade. "You just need to keep practicing."

I cup the jar. It's cool in my sweaty palms.

"But I can't stop *worrying*."

"Well, that takes practice too," she says. "Some people worry more than others. Some people probably don't worry enough. We don't get to pick the particular hand we're dealt.

But hopefully, we learn from our mistakes and we get better at managing it." She leans into my shoulder. "I love you so much, Franny. You know that, right?"

I nod and swallow. It's a lot to take in—the idea that you have to practice being yourself.

"Want to say the seven *C*s?" she asks.

"I do not."

"Fair enough."

I look up at the sky. "You can really see the stars tonight."

"That reminds me"—she reaches down for something under her chair—"of the reason I'm up here in the first place." She hands me the box tied with string. I forgot all about it.

"Go on." She nudges it on my lap. "Open it."

I untie the string and lift the lid. Inside are two embroidery hoops, the smaller one stacked on top of the other. I lift them out and hold them up to the light of the moon. Both clamp down fabric that is covered in navy blue stitches the exact same color as my dress. A thin line of white thread forms a pattern. I can't make sense of it until Mom holds them up side by side.

"Little D and Big D, remember?" she asks, and the pattern of the constellations reveals itself like the world's best puzzle.

I take them back to get a better look.

"It's not about you being like me, you know," she says while I study them. "That's not why I call you Little D."

"Why, then?"

She plucks the string that connects them with her finger.

"So you won't forget we're in this thing together."

I thought it was the money that would keep us safe. But it's this. It's me and Mom, and also Mimi and Sloan and Noah and Mrs. Ivey and everybody else, stitched together.

I look up from the stars in my hands to the ones in the sky, and my heart lifts.

ACKNOWLEDGMENTS

I WROTE THIS BOOK in my bathroom with the door shut while sitting in an empty bathtub with a pillow in my lap. I think my foot might still be asleep. The pandemic had just begun. My children were home. My husband was home. We were all suddenly so *close*, in one another's spaces, and the world felt big and frightening. This book helped me both distract myself from and also process the fear and uncertainty I felt outside that tiled room. It gave me so much. I hope it can give others a feeling of safety and bravery when they need it. Or distraction. Distraction is good too.

I have many people to thank for helping me pull this one off during that time. Jody, thank you for hanging in there with the kids when life turned upside down. And, kiddos, thank you for being your resilient, wonderfully weird selves.

Big huge whopper of a thank-you to my editor, Reka Simonsen, for handling this book with care and understanding the heart behind the story.

Many thanks to Keely Boeving, my agent, for loving Mimi and her one-liners and Sloan in all her shoulder-punching glory.

Thank you to Karyn Lee and Jacqueline Li for a gorgeous cover. The paper crane was the chef's kiss!

The entire Simon & Schuster education team always goes above and beyond to get my work into the hands of those who need it. Some of my best memories and most satisfying work trips are the conferences where we get to hang in person. You all rock.

I'd also like to thank Stephanie Land, whose incredible memoir, *Maid*, first sparked this idea of a mother and daughter trying to piece together a life as best they can.

Lastly, thank you to those in Alcoholics Anonymous, Narcotics Anonymous, and Al-Anon who were willing to share your stories with me. It was an honor.